STORKY

How I Lost My Nickname and Won the Girl

STORKY

How I Lost My Nickname and Won the Girl

BY
D. L. GARFINKLE

G. P. PUTNAM'S SONS • NEW YORK

G. P. PUTNAM'S SONS
A division of Penguin Young Readers Group
Published by The Penguin Group
Penguin Group (USA) Inc., 375 Hudson Street, New York, NY 10014, U.S.A.
Penguin Group (Canada), 10 Alcorn Avenue, Toronto, Ontario, Canada, M4V 3B2
(a division of Pearson Penguin Canada Inc.).
Penguin Books Ltd, 80 Strand, London WC2R 0RL, England.
Penguin Ireland, 25 St. Stephen's Green, Dublin 2, Ireland (a division of Penguin Books Ltd.).
Penguin Group (Australia), 250 Camberwell Road, Camberwell, Victoria 3124, Australia
(a division of Pearson Australia Group Pty Ltd)
Penguin Books India Pvt Ltd, 11 Community Centre, Panchsheel Park, New Delhi - 110 017, India.
Penguin Group (NZ), Cnr Airborne and Rosedale Roads, Albany, Auckland 1310, New Zealand
(a division of Pearson New Zealand Ltd).
Penguin Books (South Africa) (Pty) Ltd, 24 Sturdee Avenue, Rosebank,
Johannesburg 2196, South Africa.
Penguin Books Ltd, Registered Offices: 80 Strand, London WC2R 0RL, England.

Published simultaneously in Canada. Printed in the United States of America.
Design by Marikka Tamura. Text set in Stempel Garamond.
Library of Congress Cataloging-in-Publication Data
Garfinkle, Debra.
Storky : how I lost my nickname and won the girl / Debra Garfinkle. p. cm.
Summary: Fourteen-year-old Michael "Storky" Pomerantz's journal of
his freshman year of high school details his experiences,
from dealing with his mother's dating his dentist
to his attempts to win the heart of the girl he loves.
[1. Diaries—Fiction. 2. High schools—Fiction. 3. Schools—Fiction.
4. Dating (Social customs)—Fiction. 5. Family life—California—Fiction.
6. Divorce—Fiction. 7. California—Fiction.]
I. Title. PZ7.G17975St 2005 [Fic]—dc22 2004005507
ISBN 0-399-24284-8
1 3 5 7 9 10 8 6 4 2
First Impression

Dedicated to Jeff,
the best thing that ever happened to me.

ACKNOWLEDGMENTS

I'm grateful for my wonderful friends and family, especially Jeffrey Garfinkle; Sarah, Mark, and Aaron Garfinkle, my greatest achievements; Judy Green; April and Jessie Holland; Lane Klein and our book club; Micaela Alas-San Miguel; and Jeanne Taber.

Thank you to the writers I've met on the Net and in the flesh, who've been shockingly kind and helpful; my wise and fun critique group; James Meyers, my Dr. Berm, who made me revise until it hurt; and Bob Shacochis, Peggy Lang, the San Diego Book Awards Association, John H. Ritter, and Alyssa Eisner, for all their encouragement.

This book would not exist without three amazing people: Judy Reeves, who taught me how to write; Laura Rennert, who took a big dumb chance on me; and John Rudolph, whose picture is in the dictionary under *dream editor.*

And to anyone not at the A-list table in the crapeteria: You're A-list in my book!

Sunday, August 29

HOPES FOR HIGH SCHOOL

1. Gina confesses she's madly in love with me.
2. Dad teaches me to drive and buys me a Land Rover.
3. I'm the first freshman ever voted homecoming king.

REALISTIC HOPES FOR HIGH SCHOOL

1. Gina doesn't totally blow me off.
2. Dad lets me sit in the front seat of his car.
3. I don't get thrown into a Dumpster.

Monday, August 30

High school sucks rocks.

4 people at 4 separate times called me Storky today. I was hoping to lose that lame nickname. How hard is it to say Michael or Mike? It's all my fault, for being such a stork. If I looked up the word *storky* in the dictionary, I'd probably see my picture. I'm way too tall for my weight and way too thin for my height. Not to mention the bird legs and wiry hair.

Soon people won't even know my real name. They'll probably still be calling me Storky at our 20-year reunion.

I'll be in an old-age home and the nurses will call me Storky.
I can just see it on my grave:

Here Lies Storky.

3 people at 3 separate times found out my last name
today and went, "Are you *Amanda's* little brother?" like
they couldn't believe it, that I'm such a dork when she's the
Queen of Popularville.

0 people ate lunch with me today. I wish Brian was here.
Nothing like your best friend moving out of San Diego the
week before school starts. If Brian was still around, I'd be
in his kitchen right now trolling for junk food. Not sitting
in my bedroom typing this stuff on the computer about my
crappy day.

I only started this journal to have something in common
with Gina and to let her know I'm a sensitive guy. But I got
kind of addicted to it. Kind of. Like a heroin addict kind of
needs drugs.

I wonder if Gina's doing her journal right now too, using
that pink diary I gave her last year for her birthday. I can just
imagine her hunched over it, sitting cross-legged on her bed
in a little white lace nightie.

No. Better picture her fully clothed at her desk. Otherwise Rex might go nuts in my pajama bottoms and I won't
be able to concentrate on my journal. Or anything else.

Okay, now I'm imagining Gina in gray sweatpants and
a big black jacket. Oops. Not leather. Something ugly. Polyester. Good Rex.

Maybe right now Gina's twisting her hair as she writes about her perfect, nickname-less, friend-filled day. And her major crush on me. Yeah, right. Minor crush? Not even.

Sunday, September 5

Dad came 21 minutes late and took me out for Spanish food. He said, "Mercedes Bonnafeux gave this a 4-fork rating on the radio last week." And I'm like, Ugh, another foodie restaurant. I didn't say that. Just thought it. I'd rather go to a movie or bowling, so you don't have to talk so much.

We sat at the table wracking our brains for stuff to say. At least I did. He mostly chewed on octopus legs, checked out his Rolex, and watched the front door.

Finally, Dad's newest bimbo delight showed up. I call her The Thighmaster, because she's always groping Dad's leg. She makes her living getting rid of ladies' hair. Facial and pubic. That's just weird. Brian said they put hot wax over ladies' pubes, let it dry, and then pull it off. Ow! Why would anyone want to do that? I'm glad I'm not a girl. The Thighmaster's job sounds like the worst in the world, besides the guy who cleans up the animal crap at the petting zoo. And substitute teachers.

Dad managed to work in his story again about playing college football against Boomer Esiason, how he intercepted Boomer's big pass in the last quarter of the game. I can quote him on it by now. "And when I took that ball and turned it around, Boomer looked like his mother had just died on him. He's probably still not over it yet." Then he always ends with this deep chuckle.

Got to hand it to The Thighmaster though. She goes, "Who's Boomer Esiason?"

She practically sat on Dad's lap, stroking his chest while she talked nonstop. Mostly yakking about some friend who got her ankle tattooed in Tijuana. That got her lifting up her sundress to show off the Minnie Mouse tattoo on her thigh, and her and Dad giggling like morons.

That's when I started thinking about *Home Improvement*, how great it would be to live with both your parents, no sisters in the house, just working on cars every day after school with your dad while your mom made cookies.

I guess if I lifted weights, or played a sport, or at least wasn't a nerd, Dad wouldn't need his girlfriends for company on Sunday nights.

Monday, September 6

NOTE TO SELF: Memorize map of school. So you don't have to stare at it while you're walking. Because you could bump into people. Like 2 huge lardheads. And they could try to give you a wedgie. They could in fact succeed. You could still be sore 9½ hours later.

Remember to call said lardheads in 10 years if you need pool service for your humongous swimming pool with the swim-up bar and Jacuzzi. Because that's probably the kind of career they'll have. Pool men. While you'll be either the Voice of the Padres, a Humvee/Ferrari dealer, or *Playboy*'s talent scout.

Tuesday, September 7

Mom completely humiliated me at my dentist's office today. She just had to bring her Rules of Evidence flashcards into his waiting room. And she wore her USD Law T-shirt with the toothy guy chasing an ambulance on it. It wouldn't be too bad if you were 25, but not if you're 40 and all the other moms are in polo shirts or suits, reading *Good Housekeeping* and *People*. I bet she's the oldest person in her entire law school.

Then I had to see the annoying Dr. Berman. As I laid back on the chair, he put his pudgy hand through my hair and goes, "Let's take a look at those teeth, Mikey."

I don't like people messing with my hair, except girls, maybe. Plus he still calls me Mikey and I haven't been Mikey in 8 years.

But what really bugged is that after he pushed me off to his assistant, he must have headed right for Mom. When I came back to the waiting room, he goes, "Bye, Geraldine, study hard. See you Friday."

And Mom goes, "Okay, Howard, 8 o'clock." Then she giggled and thanked him for helping her with her flashcards.

Yes, my life has gotten even worse. Mom now has a date with my fat dentist.

Wednesday, September 8

Turns out Gina's going on a date too. Will my good luck streak never end?

I biked to her house after school. She looked gorgeous as usual. And patriotic. She wore this American flag halter top that was so tight the stripes were all curvy.

I stood at her door listing 2-letter Scrabble words in my head, the only way I could keep Rex calm in my Fruit of the Looms.

She went on and on about this guy who asked her out at lunch today. Gina automatically went to the A-list table the first week of high school. Since Brian moved away, I have no one to sit with. It sucks.

"He's 16," she said as I thought of *pa, pe,* and *pi.* "He has his own car." She did her adorable pout and goes, "How could he be interested in me?"

I go, "He'll love you. You were so popular in middle school, and everyone thinks you're cute." Then she smiled and said, "You think?" I wanted to be honest. To say, I think you're the most beautiful girl in the universe, and your smile is killing me. Instead I nodded and asked if she did all the Encouraged Reading.

She's like, "What?" I said, "You know, in the orientation handbook? *The Pearl, Wuthering Heights, Waiting for Godot.* I read one a week this summer."

Couldn't figure out her reaction. She just looked at me with her pretty little mouth open. Awed by Captain Sensitive? Did she think to herself, Michael Pomerantz might seem kind of dorky on the outside, but the inside is what counts, and he's the most deep, insightful, literary, just plain sensitive person I've ever met. Especially for a male. In a heterosexual way, of course. I can't wait to see what other parts of him are sensitive.

Or with my luck, Gina was merely stunned by my dweebosity. Not that I could focus on her feelings with her in that halter top.

Now I can, typing my journal. Sometimes I think the only reason me and Gina are friends is because we've been friends since fourth grade, when we were the only kids pulled out for gifted class. Which mostly meant skipping spelling tests so we could build giant molecules and play Mancala while the gifted teacher read the *National Enquirer*.

Wait. That's not the only reason Gina likes me. I'm the guy she can play Scrabble with, or use 4-syllable words around, or bitch about Honors Algebra to. She gets to act smart around me. Little does she know I keep picturing her naked.

So she told me this dude plays football and he's a junior and his nickname is Hunk. Hunk? Why not just Brute, or Hulk, or Thug? "And," Gina says, "he has the most exquisite gray eyes and really, really big calf muscles." Too much information.

I told her our football team is supposed to suck this year, even worse than last year. But that just kept her in Hunk mode, how he asked her to watch his practice, how he worked out all summer so he could make varsity, blah blah blah, and I said I had to go. A guy like me doesn't have a

chance with a girl like her. Yeah, I'm Gina's dream date—
Brillo pad hair, beak nose, and all.

Thursday, September 9

MY MOST EMBARRASSING MOMENTS IN LIFE

1. What happened today.
2. Puking on the bus up to Camp Mount Laguna.
3. Wandering into the girls' bathroom by mistake the first week of middle school.
4. When I dove into the pool at Erica Sung's swim party and my shorts fell off.
5. Crying in homeroom the day after Dad moved out.
6. Amanda walking in while I was exercising Rex.

In Honors English today, Ms. Dore was droning on about *The Great Gatsby*, how it's supposed to be this great romantic book. Yawn, yawn, yawn. All the sudden Ms. Dore shut up, walked over to Heather Kvaas, and snatched a note right out of her hand. After she read it, she marched down the aisle and gave it to me. Gina let out this loud gasp and everyone laughed. Ms. Dore went back to the chalkboard and continued droning.

Gina had written "Gina Harrison" 9 times on top of the note. Like she's going to marry Hunk Harrison and it takes so much preparation to get used to the name, she's got to write it 9 times a day. Underneath she wrote, "Heather, should I tell Mike P. (Storky) about his fly?"

I looked down and there it was, unzipped. My briefs

were poking out. One of the pairs dyed pink in the laundry last month. I shot a look at Gina, and she was totally staring at me. But she turned away as soon as I looked at her. I closed my fly so fast it's lucky Rex didn't get caught in the zipper.

How long was my fly open? All day? Through lunch? Why didn't anyone tell me? Maybe no one noticed. Who noticed, I wonder? Gina did. Why was Gina looking at my crotch anyway? Maybe that's a good thing. But she called me Storky. I hope she never ever brings this up, ever. I don't think I can talk to her for a long time. Not that we speak much anyway.

Friday, September 10

Mom's on her date. She already broke one of Amanda's Cardinal Rules of Dating. She's out with someone who didn't ask her at least a week in advance. According to my sister, asking a girl out for less than a week before is like telling her you know she has nothing else to do. If Justin Timberlake asked Amanda out for 6 days from now, she'd probably turn him down.

That's not a problem for me, considering I've never asked a girl out. And I guess it's not a problem for Amanda either, being so hot. But Mom hasn't been on one date since the Divorce, so if she said no, she might have to wait another 2 years.

Another Cardinal Rule of Dating is never let a guy be more than 15 minutes late. Twice I saw Amanda refuse to answer the door when a guy exceeded the 15-minute limit. I know I'll never be late to pick up a girl. Well, like 5 minutes late. Amanda says it's wimpy to get there exactly on time.

Dr. Vermin came 19 minutes late. Even with aftershave on, he still smelled like dental office. He wore his hair all slicked back like he'd fallen headfirst into a vat of motor oil.

I saw Aunt Marsha give Mom a thumbs-up sign behind Dr. Vermin's back. No way did he deserve that. Aunt Marsha had come over with June to help Mom get ready for the date. Supposedly. I bet they just wanted to check out Dr. Vermin.

I'm sort of used to seeing Aunt Marsha and June holding hands now. If I lost my virginity to an older woman, I'd definitely pick June. Except that she's a lesbian. Maybe she's bi though? Maybe one night with me and she'd become a total hetero? Sure.

Dr. Vermin didn't stay long. Mom made me vacuum the whole house for nothing. He just went, "Hi, everyone. Are you ready, Geraldine? You look like a queen." Mom shot Aunt Marsha a look, like, Is that good or bad? After practically taking Mom's closet apart, they had finally decided on this white pantsuit. I didn't see anything queenly about it. Not even royal. Amanda did this big phony smile and Dr. Vermin took Mom's hand and they left. At least he didn't mess with my hair again.

When they walked out, me and Amanda pretended to puke. Then everyone but me went somewhere. Aunt Marsha and June went off to see some barfy art film. Amanda had a date, of course. He came to the door looking like Ken doll's twin, in a tweed blazer and button-down shirt. When he found out Mom wasn't here, Ken doll stripped down to a Coors Mountain Brewery T-shirt and jeans and went, "Party time."

After they left, I just hung around like usual, flipping the channels between MTV and Nick at Nite. I heated up a frozen pizza and ended up eating the whole thing. I'm a pig.

I wonder when Mom's coming home.

Saturday, September 11

It's 1:33 A.M. Amanda just got back. *Before Mom.* When I told Amanda, she said in this loud voice as if Mom, wherever she was, could hear her, "Good for you, Mom, you're finally getting laid."

Laid? No way. Gross! Admittedly, it's possible. But for my own mental health, I cannot think about it.

Saturday, September 11

It's 2:14 A.M. and I'd like to know where Mom is. What if Dr. Vermin kidnapped her? I mean, how much do we know about him, really? Just that he's a dentist. That alone makes him evil.

Amanda's fast asleep, sprawled on her bed with the light on, dried drool on her chin, clutching a romance novel, *Prisoner of My Desire*. It's too bad no one in high school really knows her like I do. She's a closet geek.

I could sneak the novel out of her room. But it's too much work to go through all the descriptions of fancy dresses and sunrises just to get to the throbbing loins and hot pulsating flesh stuff.

I'm going to sit on that stupid flowery couch Mom bought right after the Divorce until she comes home. I've been flipping between TV movies: hot babe with gun avenges rape, hot babe in tight prison jumpsuit fights off lesbians, and hot babe stalked by madman slowly loses clothes.

My brain is exploding with worry about Mom, but Rex at least is happy. Especially when that hot babe's skirt got caught in the door, and to escape the madman she had to rip half of it off.

Saturday, September 11

WHAT MOM TOLD AUNT MARSHA ON THE PHONE TODAY

1. Dr. Vermin's a good listener.
2. They didn't do the deed.
3. She never thought her teenage son would be waiting up for her on a Friday night.
4. I'm all shy and still coming into myself.
5. She's meeting him for lunch on Monday.

WHAT I'D LIKE TO TELL MOM EXCEPT THEN SHE'D KNOW I WAS EAVESDROPPING

1. He's only a good listener because he wants to do the deed.
2. Thank God you didn't do the deed!
3. I never thought I'd be waiting up for my mom on a Friday night either.

4. What does coming into myself mean anyway?
5. Don't meet him for lunch Monday. Don't meet him
   again for anything ever.

Sunday, September 12

Dad took me and The Thighmaster to this Japanese-Mexican place that just opened downtown. I asked Dad if maybe we could go to a high school football game one Friday instead of out to eat or whatever on Sundays. He said, "Let's just stick to Sundays." No explanation or anything. If I played football, he'd probably sit in the bleachers every Friday wearing the school colors and tooting a giant horn.

In the middle of dinner, right when Dad had a piece of carne asada in his chopsticks, I go, "Mom stayed out all night with my dentist." I wanted to shock him. But he didn't even drop the meat. He just goes, "Oh, good for her."

No big deal to him, I guess. He's always got a bimbo delight. And Amanda says he had tons of affairs when he was married. She won't even talk to him anymore. Mostly because the marriage breaker was Amanda's assistant gymnastics coach.

If Amanda ever showed up on Sunday nights, Dad would ask her where she wanted to go. If I was popular like her, I bet he'd ask me once in a while. Maybe Dad would be all proud of me, and say, Hey, you pick the restaurant this time, and remind me to buy you a car next year so you can drive to all those parties you keep getting invited to and take your girlfriend Gina out for steak and french fries. He might call them *pommes frites*, but I'd forgive him.

Monday, September 13

Wow! A girl actually talked to me today. Not Gina, but still. A 10th grader!

I was walking out of Spanish class when it happened. This girl, Sydney Holland, goes, "Did you understand what Ms. Padilla was saying? Because I only got like half of it." And I said, "That's twice as much as I got."

It's bad enough Ms. Padilla won't use English on us, but she speaks Spanish like an auctioneer on speed. Half the time I'm sitting in a daze, hoping she didn't just say something like, Anyone who doesn't understand me will automatically fail my class.

So in the hallway Sydney Holland and I compared notes. She seems smart and very nice. Plus she has big round breasts.

Wednesday, September 15

I finally made a friend today. Nate Karnowski. I was sitting by myself in the crapeteria, and this other guy sat down diagonal to me and started reading *Waiting for Godot*. Encouraged Reading book. I figured I could either spend another lunch period staring at my tray and wishing Brian was here, or I could try to talk.

It took me 3 minutes to come up with something to say. Finally I go, "You like the book?" He smirked at me. So then I said, "I read it last month, just came out of the coma."

The smirk turned into mega-smirk and he passed the book across the table to me. Taped inside some of the pages were these playing cards with naked ladies on them. Totally naked. Except some had on necklaces or boas or hats. One wore a gold belt. Just the belt.

I smirked right back at him and said, "Great book. Where'd you get that stuff?" And he says, "Reno. My dad bought them." His dad. Cool. Which is what I said. "Cool." And he shrugged like it was no big deal and stuck out his hand to shake and goes, "Nate Karnowski, I'm in Honors English with you."

So we're friends now. He's into football too. Watching, not playing. I'm pretty sure he's a couch potato like me. We might go to the game together next week. I'd like to see the Hunk fumble the ball and lose the game, or at least get knocked on his ass real hard.

Saturday, September 18

I think everyone on the planet went on a date tonight except me. Amanda and her best friend Bulimic Michele are out with these twins who are supposedly the hottest straight guys in the whole school.

Doctor Vermin took Mom out again. I swear he smells like dental office even in our house. First thing he does is rough up my hair. Second thing he does is call me Mikey. Third thing he does is ask How's school. Lost 3 points right there, all in a row.

Mom wore a new green pantsuit that made her look like

a stalk of celery. Verm had this expression on his face. If he was a dog, he'd be panting and wagging his tail. Actually, if he was a dog, he'd be one of those smelly fat ones that always lies on the chair you wanted to sit on.

I headed toward my room. "You'll be okay?" Mom asked. She still isn't used to going out at night. I reminded her that I'm 14 already.

Then Vermin says, "You want to come with? Any movie you want to see?" I told him I liked horror flicks, just because adults never go to those. Mom sighed like I'm such a disappointment. She did that thing where she goes, "Oh, Mike," and she sounds just like Carol Brady on those rare episodes where she isn't all chipper. Mom goes, "You like other stuff too." Verm butts right in, suggesting all these movies, like he's already part of the family.

What if someone from school saw me at the movies with my mom on a Saturday night? Total patheticity. And who would want to smell that Novocain or whatever it is all night? And watch him put his chubby arm around her?

I tried to think up something polite to get out of it. Then Vermin started stroking Mom's palm with his thumb. I just said, "Nah."

After they left, I called Gina, hoping maybe the Hunk had stood her up and she'd be home. That's really mean, hoping like that. I guess I'd have felt pretty bad if she'd answered the phone all disappointed. No, I wouldn't. The phone just rang and I hung up before the 6th ring when the machine picks up.

So he probably didn't stand her up, but I still bet I'm

much more sensitive than he is. I'm Captain Sensitive. Like if I ever had a date with Gina, I'd bring flowers and/or chocolates and I'd ask her where she wanted to go. Even if she suggested some dumb Mandy Moore movie, I'd say, What a great idea.

And I bet I'm smarter than Hunk. A guy named Hunk can't be smart. My brain could probably eat his for lunch and still want dessert. I'll invite Gina over for Scrabble so she can make the Mike/Hunk brain comparison.

Sunday, September 19

Dad canceled on me tonight. Says he has a cold.

Meanwhile, Mom's been a total nag. Threatening to make me volunteer at Golden Village Retirement Home with her. She gave the old lecture about joining clubs and stuff instead of vegging around the house all day with the remote glued to my hand, feeling sorry for myself about Gina.

"Thanks for the idea of gluing the remote to my hand. Hadn't thought of that one," I said. You could just see her face burning up. I'm never having kids. We're such brats. You can almost understand why Dad moved out.

How does she know I like Gina?

Monday, September 20

Gina came over to play Scrabble. She hasn't been here in 37 days. We used to play like every weekend. Then last year she was always at someone's party or at the mall with her pretty girls group, or worst of all, at the movies with a guy.

Arranging a Scrabble game with her nowadays is an ordeal. It's worth it though.

She takes forever to put down her tiles, but that's okay. While she's frowning over them and rearranging them a zillion times, I stare at her boobs. I wonder if Gina likes them. Do they throw off her balance? Did she have to buy all new shirts?

She won the game. So much for impressing her with my brainpower. It's not really fair, because I couldn't concentrate and keep Rex under control at the same time. Just to calm him down, I had to stare at the wall and take 3 all the way to the 6th power. Then Gina swiped an eyelash off my cheek with her little hand, and Rex rose like pizza dough. I was forced to list the 13 original colonies in alphabetical order.

After the game we ate vanilla ice cream at the kitchen table. As soon as we sat down, Mom decided she had to empty the dishwasher. What a coincidence. I had my usual Godzilla-sized bowl, while Gina ate about a teaspoonful.

Out of masochism or something I asked how her date went, and that set her off. I had to hear how the Hunk brought her a rose, and about his cool truck he drove with one hand, holding hers with the other, and how he held her hand the whole time over dinner, and how she hated having a curfew.

What did she want to do with the Hunk late at night anyway? I don't want to know.

While Gina jabbered about the Hunk, Mom gave me

pity stares. At one point, Mom held this big pile of knives in her hand, like to stab Gina if she said one more stupid thing about the Incredible Hunk. I guess it's obvious I have a crush on her. Or maybe Mom read my journal.

MOM, IF YOU'RE READING THIS RIGHT NOW, I HOPE YOU KNOW YOU'RE TOTALLY VIOLATING MY TRUST AND SCREWING UP MY PSYCHE, AND IF YOU EVER DO IT AGAIN, I'LL RUN AWAY FROM HOME OR SOMETHING. ALSO, DUMP DR. BERMAN.

Thursday, September 23

In my quest to show Gina what a nice guy I am, and to get Mom to stop nagging me, and because Amanda was blaring *Bridges of Madison County* on TV tonight, I went with Mom to Golden Village.

I got to play Scrabble. Against an old geezer in a wheelchair though. Called himself Duke. His real name is probably Wilbert or something. Within the first 6 minutes, he put down two 7-letter words I never heard of. After I challenged him on *wych* and lost my turn, he did an annoying laugh involving a lot of head bobbing. I just sighed.

He said, "You seem glum." Glum. Geezer expression meaning bummed. I said, "You're kicking my butt." Then he goes, "But you seemed glum when you got here. Not that you're exactly at Disneyland." He leaned his wrinkly face into mine and said, "Don't listen when people tell you high school is the best time of your life. It's mostly crap about popularity, and jock worship, and tests on subjects you have no use for."

And I'm like, "Don't forget pimples. Zits can really make a person glum." And he nodded like one of those bobble-head dolls.

Great pep talk. But, I don't know, I guess it was good to hear someone else say high school sucked. Even an ancient guy.

He ended up winning the game. Beat me by more than 100 points. Afterward, I had to shake his hand. It felt like a peach that you forgot about in the refrigerator for 3 weeks.

Mom's pretty great, I guess, to go over there every week. Duke said if I come back, he'll give me some Scrabble tips. I don't think I have it in me.

Saturday, September 25

I'm so busted. Nate says Mom looked like she wanted to kill me on the ride home last night. But I'm still alive, so it was worth it.

What a night. Went to my first high school football game. We got there really early because Nate wanted to sit right in front of the cheerleaders. We could see their nipples all perked up in the cold air. We bought some 7UPs at the snack stand, and then Nate took out this bottle of vodka from his jacket pocket. He said he swiped it from his mom. At first I felt like my mouth was on fire, but after a few sips I sort of got used to it.

Gina sat right next to me. First she came up behind me and covered my eyes. As soon as she said, "Guess who" in her sweet high voice, I knew it was her. I said, "Principal Craterface," and Gina cracked up. When she laughed, her boobs moved up and down against my back. I think it was her boobs. I'm pretty sure I felt them.

She was dressed all cute, in this tight little furry sweater that didn't even go to her waist. And she had noisy bracelets all over her arm. She smelled like an orange grove. Either she'd just eaten a lot of citrus fruit or she had on really strong perfume. She was with Heather Kvaas, a total babe who looks like Reese Witherspoon minus the chin. Heather's like, "Don't they call you Storky?" Which nearly ruined my night until Nate said, "He's Mike to us friends," and she goes, "Okay. Mike."

Nate gave a cup to Gina. She took a gulp and said, "Ooh, Vodka and 7," like she's been drinking these things for years. I couldn't believe it was Gina.

Sydney Holland from Spanish class and another girl, Miranda something, sat behind us. Miranda whispered that we were lowlifes, and tried to get Sydney to move away from us. I like being called Lowlife. Especially compared to Storky. I like Sydney too. She's still the only 10th grader who ever said hello to me. And she's got those great breasts. Unfortunately, when Nate offered them a swig of vodka, they changed seats.

Nate and the girls downed the stuff. I didn't want to look like a wuss so I drank some too. It put me in a daze. I felt good, real happy, but like a silent slow-motion happy. I probably had this stupid grin across my face all night like those people who get picked to come on down on *The Price Is Right.*

Hunk sat on the bench the whole first half of the game. Gina goes, "I'm cold," and like a moron I gave her this little pat on the shoulder. Then Nate takes off his jacket and passes it over me to her. I wish I'd thought of that. I asked Heather if she wanted to wear my jacket, but she didn't.

Besides the jacket thing, I was thinking it was about the greatest night of my life—hanging with Nate, staring at cheerleaders bouncing around right in front of me, sitting next to Gina, who was all pink and giggly from the booze.

Things went downhill after halftime. Hunk ran onto the field and Gina started jumping like crazy. Her bracelets clanged against each other, making a racket. Very first play the quarterback throws the ball into Hunk's giant monster hands, and he runs with it 40 yards. Gina gave me a headache from screaming so much, and then the girls and Nate started chanting, "Hunk! Hunk! Hunk!" and everyone around us yelled it too.

I just sat slumped in my seat, with a jackhammer going off in my head and a blender in my stomach. Hunk's run turned into the team's only touchdown. It didn't really help, since we lost 27-6. But it still made Hunk the big star of our lame team.

Gina tossed Nate his jacket and ran toward the field as soon as the game ended, with Heather following after her. Nate goes, "I'm in love." And I said, "Gina's mine." She wasn't, she isn't, she never was. But a drunk guy can dream, right?

Then Nate said, "I mean Heather. She's hot." And I nodded, which powered up the jackhammer inside my head.

I kept stumbling as I made my way out of the bleachers. I fell once, onto what looked like 2 irate state wrestling champions or maybe 1 national champ. Everything was blurry. I think the only reason I didn't get killed is because Nate told him/them I was about to blow chow. I owe him big.

The setting for my stomach blender had sped up to pulverize and the bathroom was like 100 people away. So I lurched through the parking lot to the nearest trash can and puked my guts out. Nate caught up with me, laughed, and called me a lightweight.

About 30 seconds after that, Sydney Holland appeared. She threw an empty Raisinets box into the trash can, then pinched her nostrils shut and waved off the stench. "That's disgusting," I said. "Who did that?" She either glared at me or winked at me—I was too blotto to tell—before walking away. I hope it was a wink. If Sydney Holland knew I ralphed, she'd definitely think I was a lowlife.

When we got into Mom's car she was so excited that I had this new friend and was finally doing a school activity that at first she didn't even get that I was drunk. Then she started asking her usual gazillion questions. What was the score, who was there, was it crowded? After a while, she said, "You don't seem yourself tonight." I said, "I feel sick." She goes, "Tell me about it." But it wasn't her concerned parental voice. It was her lawyer-in-training voice, waiting for me to break down and admit I'm a drunk loser disappointment of a son.

I said something about the stomach flu, and she said, "Stomach flu, my ass," which nearly sobered me up since she never talks like that. She must have been really pissed at me. Or maybe her date with Vermin tanked. Hopefully. At the next stoplight, she put her face up to mine, sniffed my breath, and goes, "You're in big trouble, mister."

My headache didn't even go away until around noon today. Last night Mom said she'd think of a punishment and get back to me. Whatever.

Sunday, September 26

Mom hid the TV! I can't believe it! When she went to the law library today, I searched the garage, every closet, all over Mom's bedroom. Maybe it's in her car. I bet it's there. I'll look in the trunk first thing tomorrow.

Amanda wouldn't even help me. I'm like, "Don't you want the TV back? Tell Mom it's not fair 'cause you didn't do anything wrong." And she goes all snobby, "I don't have time for TV. I have a social life." When I said I did too, she laughed in my face.

I have absolutely nothing to do tonight. Dad canceled on me again. Said he had to take care of an important client. The Thighmaster was giggling in the background.

I'm so bored. We're not even hooked up to the Net anymore. Why did Dad get to take the good computer? It's not fair. There's only 1 of him and 3 of us. We had to take Aunt Marsha's lame hand-me-down doorstop. All I can do on this lousy thing is play ancient computer games, do homework, and type this journal.

At least I read *To Kill a Mockingbird* today. Awesome book. Are there really fathers like that out there?

Monday, September 27

The TV's not in the car. Mom won't let me have it for 3 weeks. She says it's not just a punishment for getting drunk. It's supposed to make me a better person. That's so wacked. I hate when people do nasty stuff to you and pretend it's for your own benefit.

I could go to Nate's. He says he has 4 TVs in his house— 1 in his mom's room, a big-screen TV in the living room, 1 in the den, and 1 in his bedroom. He's also got a wireless hookup. And he didn't even get in trouble for drinking last week. He says when he got home from the football game, his mom was passed out on the couch and didn't even notice him come in.

Thursday, September 30

Today Gina actually flagged me down in the hallway at school. She whispered that we should play Scrabble again soon, and then she asked me to summarize *A Farewell to Arms*. She's like, "You're so good in English, and I didn't get the chance to read it in depth."

Michael A. Pomerantz, alias Captain Sensitive, saves the

day! I told her all about the book. It was a pretty decent read. Especially the war stuff. Gina made me late to history class, but she's definitely worth it.

Sunday, October 3

Maybe I'd get along better with Dad if I didn't think about the Divorce so much. About them arguing, or him moving out, or any of that stuff. Maybe he'd talk to me more if I wasn't walking around mad at him all the time.

I should be happy Dad let me hang out at his apartment tonight. Of course, that was only after he found out Le Quiche was closed for a private party. I should be happy we got to watch the Chargers game on TiVo and have leftover pizza, even if it was topped with pineapple and artichoke hearts. I should be happy he let me eat on his black leather couch. Though he was all paranoid about the crumbs.

Which made me remember this fight I started between him and Mom a few months before he moved out. Dad grounded me for eating on the couch, and Mom called him anal-retentive, and he called her a slob, and Mom said Dad was never home to sit on the couch anyway, and Dad said that was because Mom always nagged at him. Me and Amanda sat on the couch, me still with the plate of cold mac and cheese on my lap, both of us staring at the TV, not looking at Mom and Dad. I know I hate them being divorced, but maybe I hated them being married even more.

No I didn't. Or else I wouldn't have tried to get sick. That time I took a shower and then ran into my bedroom without drying off, standing totally bare-assed against the open window in a grand plot to catch pneumonia and re-unite my parents in the hospital. Picturing them on each side of the bed, holding hands over me, looking all concerned. And me finally getting well, knowing that Mom and Dad fell back in love, just like in the movies.

I never did catch pneumonia though. It's not like it gets that cold in San Diego, even in the winter. Anyway, Mom and Dad would probably just yell at each other in the hospital, or maybe Dad would visit me there on Sunday nights and Mom would get the rest of the week. All that happened from standing butt-naked against the window was that Mom got a call from Mrs. Ridsdale next door saying I flashed her.

Tonight Dad hardly saw any of the football game with me. After finishing his pizza, he left me on the couch and moved to the little table off the kitchen, paying bills and then talking to The Thighmaster on the phone, begging her to come over.

He probably hates that I'm such a slug. Especially compared to how he was in high school, the big football star/basketball team captain/homecoming king. I need to try out for a sport. Something cool, to make Dad proud.

Monday, October 4

Aced my first history quiz *and* my first Spanish essay. When she handed the papers back, Ms. Padilla said I showed a lot of sensitivity.

A jerk in the back row goes, "Dorky Storky," which made at least half the class laugh. Until Sydney Holland turned around and said she was sick of immature boys who are jealous of sensitive men like me. Some other girls went, "Yeah" and "You big idiots."

It would be excellent if the guys actually were jealous of me. Like if they all wanted to be Captain Sensitive too. Me and the other sensitive guys would be in the A-list group, and everyone would be dying to sit at our lunch table. Of course, being so sensitive, we'd hate to exclude anyone. So we'd just declare every table in the crapeteria A-list, even though mine would be known as genuinely A-list.

If only. After class I walked Gina to her locker and sensitively mentioned my volunteer trip to Golden Village with Mom. She looked at me like I was Nerdzilla. She goes, "Are you already worried about your extra-curriculars for college?" When I told her it's just to be nice, her little nose wrinkled up. Then she called out, "Hunk! Hunk!" and ran after him, flicking me a wave.

Tuesday, October 5

Today Mom gave me the choice of washing all the windows or going to Golden Village.

That Duke dude kicked my skinny butt again at Scrabble. I can't believe *dhootie* and *atlatl* are words. He said I didn't look so glum today, so I told him about getting my first A's in high school.

He said, "I bet you made your mother proud." We both

looked at her, reading this Jackie Collins book to a group of ladies smacking their lips and twirling their hair. When she caught our stares, she beamed at me like I was Gandhi. If only Gina was impressed. I told Duke, "Mom's happy about the grades. A lot of girls in my Spanish class think it's cool."

He shook his head. At first I thought it was like Parkinson's or some old-guy thing. But then he goes, "High school girls don't think good grades are cool. Trust me."

Wednesday, October 6

I'm already getting the rep for brains, 38 days into the school year. Today Sydney Holland copied my notes from Spanish class.

I wonder who has it worse in high school: me, a smart guy who's skinny and doesn't do sports, or Sydney, a smart girl with braces who doesn't wear makeup?

She does have excellent breasts though. Today she leaned over to squint at the handwriting in my notebook, and the left one plopped on top of the desk like a baby seal on the rocks at La Jolla Cove. Very playful. Her gazongas more than compensate for the braces and lack of makeup.

And actually, you can see girls' eyes better when they don't have gunk on them. What do you call the color of Sydney's eyes? Not kelly green. Definitely not lime. Army green, I guess.

After she copied my notes, she goes, "Hope you didn't mind I said that stuff Monday about being sensitive."

Mind? Is she crazy? I told her it was okay, not letting on

how she totally made my day. Heather green? Is that even a color? Moss green? Maybe ivy green. I don't know. Nice-looking green. Very.

Thursday, October 7

Tried out for the wrestling team today. Figured that's a macho enough sport to impress Dad. Last night I even pictured him and the rest of the school rooting for me as I kept pinning down helpless-looking guys on the mat.

What actually happened is a series of smelly ogres kept twisting my limbs like I was Gumby and lying on top of me while Coach Maxwell laughed and shook his head until I half crawled out of the gym.

My neck hurts and I think one of those sweatmonsters gave me a rash.

Friday, October 8

I don't like being lied to, but I can understand it in Nate's case. I've bugged him for weeks to let me come over and watch TV, and he kept putting me off. Finally, today, he said I could come. I figured out right off why he stalled before. He doesn't have 4 TVs. He doesn't have a big-screen TV. He doesn't even have a den. He lives in this little one-story house across the street from 7-Eleven, with one medium-sized TV. I didn't say anything about it and neither did he.

We watched MTV for a while, plus this *Elimidate* episode where the guy got to play beach volleyball with

4 girls in bikinis. Nate liked the tall blonde, but my vote went to the one with the biggest boobs.

Nate's mom smokes and the whole house reeks. When she drove me home in this old Ford Escort, she smoked with the windows barely open. She hardly said anything the whole way.

It's so different with Mom. She's such a griller. As soon as I got in the door, she asked all these questions about Nate and his house and school and stuff. She even asked if I'd been smoking. Ever since she caught me drinking, she's all paranoid. I bet Nate's just kicking back in front of the computer by himself now. No one bugging him.

Sunday, October 10

I bowled a 205 tonight! A new record for me! I should thank The Thighmaster. Though it was my idea. She wanted to go to some raw-food restaurant. Gross. So I said, "Did you know 3 games of bowling burn off 500 calories?" I made that up. Really I was thinking this is the one sport I'm decent at, and maybe Dad will think I'm cool for a change. I told The Thighmaster, "They serve salad at the bowling alley, so you can burn calories *and* eat raw foods." And I could eat a cheeseburger and fries instead of carrot sticks and wheat germ. After I told her and Dad that bowling's supposed to be the newest trend, they finally said okay.

I owe my 205 score to The Thighmaster breaking her nail and getting all bent out of shape early in the second game. She sat on the bench, took off one of the rental shoes, and flung it at Dad. She goes, "I refuse to do this. You drag me to these horrid places on Sundays and I can't take it anymore."

I figured Dad would tell her to grow up, or call a cab for her. But he sat next to her patting her knee and told me, "Let's go." He said, "I'll take you to my apartment and you can watch TV." The Thighmaster held out her hand and stared at her broken nail as if her finger had been chopped off. Dad leaned over and kissed it.

I wanted to say, I refuse to do this too. I refuse to listen to your bimbo delight whine about wearing geeky shoes. I refuse to wait while you get all those different balls for her before she finds one she likes. I refuse to watch you grope each other every time you pick up a spare or whenever she doesn't get a gutter ball.

I wanted to tell him, Sunday is supposed to be my night. Am I such a loser you can't spend a few hours with me by yourself? But I thought, Maybe I am. Or maybe he thinks I am. So I just said, "Can we at least finish this game?"

Me and The Thighmaster both crossed our arms and stared at Dad while he sat between us, looking scared. Finally, he shoved some money at her and suggested she get something to drink. He says all meekly, "Why don't we just stay until the end of this game?"

She glared at me like she hated my guts. I kept staring at Dad, and he got up and rolled his ball right into the gutter. The Thighmaster went over to the bar and asked for a light beer with a double shot of vodka.

After that I was so pissed, I kept imagining her bony little face in front of the pins. I started getting strikes. Later, when I calmed down some, I thought, Hey, this is a great strategy, and I switched to picturing Dr. Vermin's fat chipmunk head. But that didn't do it for me. I missed a spare. Then I pictured Hunk in his stupid tank top and got 3 strikes in a row. Next time I get mad I'm going back to the bowling alley and try to break 205.

Dad didn't even seem impressed. Mostly he was just trying to rush through the game so we could leave and The Thighmaster would stop sulking.

The good thing about seeing Dad is that Mom doesn't throw a lot of questions at me afterward like she does when I go anyplace else. So I told her I bowled a 205, and she's like, "Terrific."

I started to go upstairs to my room. Then Mom calls out, "Dr. Berman's coming over for dinner on Tuesday. I expect you and Amanda to be there."

I didn't even turn around, didn't even answer. I just climbed up the stairs and slammed my door.

Tuesday, October 12

I can't believe it. Turns out old Verm is cooler than I thought. Or maybe I got bribed from the ice cream he brought over. Mom and Amanda each got flowers. When he handed the bouquet to her, Amanda goes, "Nice touch," and just drops it on the kitchen counter. If I did that, I'd probably lose the TV another 3 weeks.

Mom fell all over herself thanking him and putting the bouquets in water and setting them on the table. Amanda sat on the couch reading *A Secret Splendor*.

Dr. Verm goes to me, "I got flowers for you too." I didn't know what to say, so I just stared at him. Then he goes, "Nah," and shows me the Ben & Jerry's bag and messes with my hair. What idiot told him teenagers like getting their heads rubbed?

I thought things would go bad, but they didn't. It's because of Mom's stupid cabbage soup diet. Why she suddenly cares about her weight is beyond me, since Vermin is like 250 pounds easy. But all she's been eating for the last 3 days is this stinky red soup.

She wasn't going to make the rest of us eat that crap. Especially not Verm. She cooked her Company Dinner, sweet-and-sour chicken, rice, asparagus, and salad. We sat around all awkward, Dr. Vermin asking me and Amanda the usual adult questions—what grade are you in, what classes are you taking, blah blah blah—and we mostly gave one-word answers.

Then when everyone was almost done eating, Mom cut one. A real loud fart, mondo strong. Easy to tell who it was too. Mom's ears turned bright red and she stared down at her food while the rest of us looked around the table.

Finally Verm goes, "My God, Geraldine, what did you put in that chicken?" He started laughing, and then Amanda and I busted up. Mom ran from the table, going, "I'm so embarrassed, excuse me, I'm so sorry." Then Verm said, "I can't eat with this smell," and he got up too, opened the window and sat on the couch.

Me and Amanda practically had to crawl to the couch, we were cracking up so bad. Then Mom came in with the Floral Fantasy Lysol from the bathroom and sprayed around the table like crazy. She was laughing too. Dr. Verm went over to Mom and put his arm around her, and that's when Amanda and I stopped laughing.

Mom told Verm I bowled a 205 on Sunday. He's in a league. His highest is 226. I guess Mom thinks since we have something in common, now we can be total pals. Yeah, right. Dr. Vermin could be worse though. I mean, compared to The Thighmaster he's fantastic.

Saturday, October 16

Gina called to have me summarize *Huckleberry Finn* before the English test Monday. She said that the Hunk took her to the Outback Steakhouse last night and held her hand all through dinner again and that it was starting to bug. She goes, "It's hard to eat with only one hand, and I wish I'd ordered something easier than steak."

I went into Captain Sensitive mode. Told her I ate steak last night too, but with both hands, and I could see how she'd be having problems. I must seem so nice and understanding to Gina compared to the Hunk. Although girls might not like guys who are nice and understanding. Maybe I should act like a jerk.

Sunday, October 17

Dad said he can't make it tonight because he has an upset stomach. How lame. Who cares anyway.

At least Duke was glad to see me after I biked over to Golden Village. Today he asked how I could be so glum when my own mother looked so happy. I go, "It's because she's seeing this jerk." When he asked what made him a jerk, I had to think awhile before I said, "He's fat and he's a dentist." Then Duke smiles and goes, "And he's not your father." I told him he's a hair ruffler. But Duke just did that big head-shaking laugh and used *festoon* to get rid of all his letters and win another game.

Monday, October 18

The TV is here! I wonder where Mom stashed it all month. When I woke up this morning, I was like those kids in the dorky Christmas commercials, bounding down the stairs, all set to maul their presents. I ripped through the channels with the remote, catching cartoons, MTV, a Hot Babe Exercise Show. Awesome.

Then, just to ruin my morning, Gina and Hunk stood at the front gate of school kissing like he was going off to war, his big monster hands planted on her little butt. It was so gross. I'm embarrassed for her. No, I'm not. I'm jealous.

But at least she can talk to me. At least we have things in common, like Scrabble and journal writing and being gifted.

What do her and Hunk ever talk about? Maybe they don't. Maybe they just make out all the time.

Tuesday, October 19

I hate school. Duke better be right about high school not being the best time of my life. If it is, then life sucks. At lunch today, I went to the bathroom and Stretch Barron stood inside the doorway totally blocking me. His stupid hairy basketball friends leaned on the dirty walls behind him, passing a big thermos around. I bet anything there was booze in there. He goes, "Seniors only, kid."

I had to walk all the way to the other side of school. I couldn't go to the bathroom near the admin building, since that's where Joey Hawkins got beat up last week and some sophomore got dunked headfirst in the toilet.

I finally made it to a bathroom I could enter without fearing for my life. Then some guy I don't know at all said, "Hey, Storky" on his way out. And just as I got some relief, right at eye level someone had written, "Amanda Pomerantz is a total tease." You really don't want to be looking at graffiti about your sister while you're trying to take a whiz.

It got me wondering if maybe Amanda is a virgin. But she can't be. She's so popular and she goes out with so many guys and I've seen her kissing them by our front door lots of times. Then I started thinking what a perv I was just wondering about my sister that way. Then I thought I better remember to zip my fly, so I did and got out of there. I hate school.

Wednesday, October 20

I feel like a hero. I got to school early today, snuck a thick black marker into that bathroom, and blackened out Amanda's name from the stall. I didn't even tell her about it. Captain Sensitive strikes again. Then, I couldn't help it, I wrote M.P.+ G.G. on the wall. I'm sick.

Friday, October 22

It's Friday night and I hung with my mother and her boyfriend all night. Pathetic.

Mom and Dr. Vermin were supposed to take line-dancing lessons tonight at this country-and-western bar. Mom's idea. Stuff like that makes me know where I get my dorkiness from. She wore Amanda's plaid shirt and these new overalls that made her look like a scarecrow. Adults shouldn't wear overalls. Unless they're genuinely doing farmwork. Just like teenagers shouldn't wear polyester unless they work in a fast-food restaurant.

Dr. Verm didn't dress up at all. He must have khakis in every shade of beige ever made. That's all he ever wears. Plus he had on a polo shirt, which is the other thing he always wears. I was hoping the cowboys at the bar would kick his ass for being such a Biff.

Soon as he saw me he went, "Hi, Mikey" and lunged for my hair. I ducked out of the way, and he ended up rubbing the air. He goes, "Just trying to say hey," and I go, "It's annoying." Verm did one of those isn't-he-cute chuckles that makes you want to punch the person. "You don't like when I mess with your hair, Mikey?" he asks. I told him I hate it, and my name is Mike, not Mikey. He did that laugh again and slapped me on the back in a way I guess he thought would make me feel macho. It was just extremely irritating.

Then Mom comes in with her piece of paper showing her cell phone number and his. Like I'm going to call them ever.

As Mom and Verm were leaving, the cordless phone rang. Mom's like, "I have to answer it in case it's Amanda." Amanda was out with this senior with a shell on his truck. Motel 6 on Wheels. Mom says hello, and then, "Calm down, Marsha, what happened?" I'm thinking maybe Grandma died, but as I listened more, I got that June dumped her. Sad.

Verm said, "This is going to be a long one." He sat next to me on the couch. *Animal House* was on, so we watched John Belushi do his zit imitation. Verm goes, "This is such a classic, I bet I've seen this movie 10 times." In the kitchen Mom kept telling Aunt Marsha to calm down while me and Dr. Vermin laughed our heads off in the living room.

It sort of reminded me of when I was 9, before the Divorce, and we all went to see the Harlem Globetrotters. Dad and I almost fell off our seats we thought it was so funny, but Amanda and Mom just sat there yawning. I remember we shared this huge carton of smelly nachos. Dad would point at one of the Globetrotters spinning the ball on his head or dribbling the ball between his legs a million miles per hour and go, "Look at that, Champ," or, "How does he do that, Champ?" I don't know when he stopped calling me Champ. I'm just Mike now.

Of course, laughing on the couch with Verm isn't the same as laughing with Dad. But anyway, it felt kind of good. I knew Verm was happy to be there too, compared to line dancing.

But I still think he's a jerk. And not just because he's probably boinking Mom. I forgot to tell Duke about Verm smelling like dental office and calling me Mikey. When he finds that out, he'll have to agree Verm's a jerk.

It took Mom about a half hour to hang up from Aunt Marsha's phone call. She asked Verm to go dancing, but he said it was too late and he wanted to see the final parade scene, which is the funniest part of the movie. Mom watched it with us, but she just smiled and shook her head while me and Verm were practically doubled over.

When it ended, Verm said we should all go to Baskin-Robbins. I almost said yes. But then I thought they'd probably hold hands in there, and I'd have to watch them be all flirty. So I said no, I'm tired. Then Mom runs into the kitchen and pulls out the ice cream.

It wasn't too bad hanging out with them. Actually, pretty decent. Verm even asked me to join his bowling league. But that's where I draw the line.

Saturday, October 23

Totally bummed. I wish Gina hadn't left ⅔ of the way through our Scrabble game. Just finished putting it away by myself. Which is really hard. Usually Gina holds the bag and I pick up the board and dump the letters in. Without someone holding the bag it takes a lot longer. Maybe she'll call me tomorrow and apologize. I thought she would tonight. She's probably out with Hunk. So much for my grand plan of using my Scrabble skills to get her all excited.

She and Amanda are the only people at school who know I play Scrabble. Some guys hide *Playboy* magazines under their beds. I hide my Scrabble dictionary. It's so geeky to make lists of good words. That list of *q* words with no *u* in them is really helpful though. I used *qat* and *qaid* today against Gina.

She played Scrabble with the Incredible Hunk last week. From how Gina told it, I could tell he sucked. Gina said he just wasn't concentrating enough. Sure. I bet she played easy on him too. Whenever she mentions him, she gets this huge smile that stays on the whole time she's talking. Her upper lip hardly moves. It's weird.

I guess I could see how a girl could think he's a hunk. He's always wearing those tank tops showing off his monster muscles. I hate guys who wear tank tops. When I see a guy wearing a tank top, I know he thinks he has a great body. He's got big white teeth too. Dr. Vermin would love him.

Where was I? So when this whole thing started, I thought it was my lucky day. Gina wore my favorite red shorts, and I had a 7-letter word, *quivers*, with room for it to go up to the triple word square. The *q* alone was worth 30 points. You can't ask for more.

I had to wait for Gina to take her turn. She took a real long time. Even for her. And it's hard sitting with a 7-letter word like that and waiting your turn. So I go, "I hope you're not as slow with the Hunk as you are with me."

She got all offended. She goes, "What do you mean by that?" in a way that would have sounded bitchy if her voice wasn't so high and squeaky. I told her it was just a stupid joke, but she said it's not funny. I go, "I just wanted you to hurry." Then she said, really angry, "Everyone's trying to hurry me all the time. Can't I just sit in a truck or think about my Scrabble game? Why can't anyone wait anymore?"

We've played about 100 games of Scrabble at least, and I've asked her to hurry up only about 10 times. And she always plays slow. I thought I was very patient. So then I said in a very patient way, "I'm sorry. Take as much time as you want."

That's when she started crying. Not like loud crying. I could just see these tears dripping down her cheeks and her little hands trying to wipe them away really fast, like if she could only get them off her face quick enough, I wouldn't notice.

Before I could figure out whether to turn my head away or hug her or what, she stood up and said, "I have to go home." I sat there, nodding. It was just so weird. One minute she's fine, joking about school, and the next second she's crying because I asked her to hurry up.

I never even got to show her I had *quivers* over a triple

word spot. Now she probably won't believe I really had it. Although I doubt I'll ever bring this up. It's too weird.

Sunday, October 24

I'm so sick of Dad. He and The Thighmaster are on this big health kick together, so we had to go to Veggie Heaven, which tastes even worse than its name. I don't know if there's a heaven, but I'm positive there aren't any veggies in it.

The whole time I had to listen to The Thighmaster lecture about the calories in everything. Which actually was pretty impressive in a wacked way. She knew the exact calorie count of every food.

At home afterward, as I polished off the leftover spaghetti and meatballs, I told Amanda that The Thighmaster was just like a strand of spaghetti, except skinnier and with less brains. Amanda goes, "It really bothers you, doesn't it? Dad always bringing someone along." "Yeah," I said. "It bugs." She goes, "Tell him." I explained how I couldn't, because his bimbo delight's always there with her hand attached to Dad's thigh, and it would just start a huge fight. Amanda goes, "Call him up."

Mom didn't say anything. She just sat at the kitchen table biting her nails and looking at the Tax Code. One of those psychological books she's always reading must say to stay out of stuff between your kids and your ex. I'm sure she was just dying. It has to be torture for her to stay quiet for so long. I appreciate it, I guess.

I think I will phone him. Tell him how I feel. In a mature way. I'll be Captain Sensitive, all polite and calm, and just say I'd like some one-on-one with you.

Maybe I should call Gina too. But what would I tell her? I'm sorry for making you cry by telling a joke? I promise to never kid around again? I should just concentrate my microscopic ability to communicate on the Dad call.

Monday, October 25

PROPOSED CALL TO DAD

1. Dad? (Hello. How are you. No, nothing's wrong. Blah blah blah.)
2. I was hoping we could have more time together on Sunday nights.
3. Dad, stop choking over the phone. I didn't mean you'd have to pick me up any earlier. I meant more one-on-one time.
4. Your girlfriend seems very nice. (Puke.)
5. But when there's more than just us, me and you don't seem to bond very well. (*Mesh? Relate?* Too new-agey?)
6. Would it be possible just to see you by yourself this Sunday? (Without the bimbo delight.)

Yeah, that sounds good. I think I'll use the word *bond*. He's into that psyche stuff. I remember him talking about Bonding as a New Kind of Family when he said he was moving out. Even then, when I was 12, I thought it sounded like bull. I'll definitely call him tomorrow.

Tuesday, October 26

I have to call Dad. By tomorrow afternoon. As soon as I get home from school. I have to get this off my chest. Besides, if I can get the Dad situation cleared up, maybe I won't be such a wuss about apologizing to Gina.

Thursday, October 28

Went to Nate's house tonight. He asked if I wanted to smoke pot. That's all I need—something that turns me all quiet and makes me want to eat a lot. I'm already quiet and I already eat a lot. He was cool about it when I said no.

If I was stoned now, I wouldn't be so pissed at myself for not calling Dad.

Friday, October 29

I admit it. I'm too much of a wimp to call Dad. So I wouldn't be a total wuss, I called Gina. She was out. Of course. It's Friday night. Everyone's out except me.

I wonder what it's like to have sex. Not necessarily with Gina, but just to have sex with a girl. Preferably Gina though. I don't really understand how you're supposed to go all in and out of a girl unless you're an acrobat or something. Plus, doesn't it hurt the girl to have some guy bouncing around on top of her? Especially Gina, with her little bones.

Maybe not someone like Sydney Holland, who's on the swim team. Sydney's arms look really solid. Her legs are probably strong too. I bet she has great legs. Maybe sex is like doing the butterfly stroke without water. I never learned that one though. I can barely do the crawl. Sydney could go on top.

I'm a perv. Mom better not be reading this journal.

Saturday, October 30

Gina called back. I apologized for making that joke last Saturday, and then she finally apologized to me. She said she was all stressed, but wouldn't tell me why.

She would have told me a few years ago. She even used to read me parts of her journal over the phone. She said I was a great listener. Even as a kid, I was a budding Captain Sensitive. That's when we were good, true friends.

Sunday, October 31

I'm sitting at the computer practically shaking. I don't know who I'm more mad at, Dad or Amanda. Or myself. I should have called Dad last week instead of putting it off. I hope Amanda gets into one of those faraway colleges she applied to. I can't handle living with her one more year.

First, Dad picked me up 23 minutes late. He honks the horn and there's The Thighmaster, sitting in the front seat of his Lexus, waving like a Rose Bowl queen. Why does she always get the front? I can't wait until Dad teaches me to drive and the bimbo delights get the backseat.

She clamped her hand on his thigh the whole time. She has these really long fake nails. Everything about her is fake. Dyed hair, phony personality, probably little plastic boobs too.

Dad tried to start a conversation. "How's school? You still friends with Gina? You ever hear from that friend of yours who moved away?" He couldn't even remember Brian's name. We only hung out together like every weekend for 4 years. When we hit the usual long pause, Dad turned on the radio to a football wrap-up show. The whole time I was thinking, Why am I here?

He goes, "We decided to eat at this seafood restaurant Mercedes Bonnafeux recommended on the radio yesterday." We? I thought, Who's we? Dad and The Thighmaster are the we. Not Dad and me.

I said, "I went out for seafood for lunch." Which isn't a lie. I had a tuna sandwich at Nate's house. We also ate the whole bag of miniature Snickers that was supposed to be for the trick-or-treat kids tonight. Nate's mom will be pissed off.

Dad says, "Oh, where did you eat?" I go, "A place called Nathan's." The Thighmaster says, "I never heard of it," like accusing me of lying. I said, "It's really small and it's in a bad area." Which is true too.

When I suggested going to the Jim Carrey movie instead, he had to look over at The Thighmaster before he said okay. I don't remember him ever looking at Mom that way.

The Thighmaster started whining about how hungry she was, and how she couldn't eat in the theater because hot dogs had all these nitrates in them and the popcorn wasn't air popped, and on and on until she made Dad stop at Submarina. Then we had to hear how fattening subs were if you used mayonnaise and cheese. The whole time I kept saying over and over to myself, Why am I here?

The fight started at the new 14-plex at the mall, but I was pretty pissed off before then. By the time we got there, the Jim Carrey movie had sold out. If we could have just bought hot dogs in the theater, or eaten afterward, we'd have gotten in and everything would have been okay. Or sort of okay.

I suggested the James Bond movie. But The Thighmaster wanted to see this stupid movie I never heard of. The poster called it the most passionate film of the year. Dad goes, "His mom doesn't want him seeing R-rated movies." Then The Thighmaster goes, "Screw his mom." That's what she said, Screw his mom. What a bitch!

I didn't say anything, because I thought Dad would yell at her. Instead he broke into this big explanation of how he and Mom are trying to respect each other, blah blah blah. He went on so long, pretending to be so understanding, we had to step out of the ticket line.

Then he suggests, like it's this brilliant idea, that I could see the James Bond movie and he and The Thighmaster could watch the passionate film and we could meet in the lobby afterward.

That did it. I walked away. Dad started walking after me,

so I ran. He called, "Mike, Mike," and I kept running. Out of the theater. Through the mall. I just ran. I tried to think what to do—go back, call someone, yell at Dad—but really I couldn't think at all. I just kept running. I ran and ran, until it dawned on me that most of the stores were closed and nobody was around, and I got kind of spooked.

I stopped. I was almost to the end of the mall. There was a McDonald's at the very end so I went in there. I ordered 2 Big Macs, then realized I only had $2. Does anything ever go right for me? I got a Sprite instead.

I sat in a booth in the back, sipping my Sprite, thinking about Dad calling, "Mike, Mike" as I ran away, and I started to smile. I was thinking, I hope he looks all over for me. I hope he leaves The Thighmaster in front of the theater while he goes to every store in the mall. I hope he has to call Mom and explain what happened.

Then I realized Mom wasn't home. She was at Dr. Vermin's supposedly studying. Then I wondered how I'd get home.

I tried to think who I knew that drove besides Mom. Aunt Marsha, but I knew she'd tell Mom everything. There was Grandma, but she's such a Dad fan, she'd probably haul me back to the movie theater. I couldn't think of anyone else but Amanda, so that's who I called. When I told her, all she said was, "That bastard! I'll be right there."

She must have left the house as soon as we hung up. It only took her 8 minutes to get to the McDonald's. Right after Amanda came in, Dad showed up. He didn't seem out of breath or anything. It was like he'd been strolling around the mall, thinking, Wouldn't it be nice if he should happen to bump into me? When Dad saw me, he gave me this tiny smile, but then he saw Amanda and looked totally thrilled.

It didn't even seem to faze her. She just laid into him. She goes, "You can't even sit next to him at the movies one day a week. He just wanted one-on-one time with you, Dad, that's all." She says, "He can't talk to you because one of your girlfriends is always around. He had to write down what he wanted to say, he wrote it all out, and then he couldn't even face calling you."

Dad didn't say much. Just that it was no excuse to make him chase me through the mall and make everyone miss the movie. Amanda went off on him so much, maybe he couldn't say everything he wanted to. Though he could have said he was sorry. He could have fit that in.

I didn't like Amanda butting in. It was my problem. She has plenty of her own problems with Dad. People at Mc-Donald's were staring at us. Even this homeless guy who probably sees plenty of strange stuff stared at us.

Then I realized Amanda must have read my journal. It's the only place I wrote down what I wanted to tell Dad. All this time I worried Mom was reading it. I never thought Amanda cared what her geeky little brother was writing.

I couldn't yell at her at McDonald's. I was too weirded out to talk. My head was pounding like a gong had gotten stuck inside it. I could barely think. So I said, "Just take me home, Amanda," and she did.

In the car she went on and on about what a pig he is. At first she yelled about it and then she started crying. She brought up the assistant gymnastics coach, how she used to spot Amanda during the day and screw Dad at night, how she made small talk with Mom when she picked Amanda up from practices, all the time doing it with Dad behind everyone's back.

I was mad about her reading my journal, but also sorry for her with her crying and everything, and grateful that she came to get me and said she wouldn't tell Mom. With Gina crying last week, and now Amanda, I see even popular people have problems—not as many as us dweebs have, I'm sure, but they have problems too.

I can't write about this anymore. I'm tired. My hands hurt from typing all this. I feel too crappy to go all over it again. I'll finish tomorrow.

Monday, November 1

I'm still so pissed at Amanda. How dare she read my journal? I deleted all the entries today. I only have the hard copies now, hidden in the middle of my box of comic books.

She must have read about me crossing out that graffiti about her. Oh, crap, and now she knows I like Gina, and all my perverted secrets.

So I have to figure out what to do not only about Dad, but also about Amanda sneaking into my journal. Plus I have to give an oral report next Monday in Honors English. Ms. Dore is making each person stand up in front of the class and recite a poem and explain it. Like she figured out everyone's worst nightmare. I never get poetry. Like that one about the rose that everybody else in the class knew was about sex, except me. I thought it was just about a rose. Plus this Friday there's those geometry and history midterms I haven't studied for.

I'm going to spend all my time this week studying. I won't even let myself think about Dad or Amanda. I'll be totally focused on English, geometry, and history. I'll even be too busy to write in this journal.

Tuesday, November 2

Couldn't study today with my brain crammed with Dad thoughts. Told myself there's still Wednesday and Thursday.

So I biked over to see Duke. He goes, "You score a perfect 10 on the glumness scale today." I didn't feel like telling him about Dad. I mean, I did feel like it in a way, but I couldn't. It's embarrassing when your own father thinks you're a loser. The whole thing of running through the mall just seems lame now. So I told Duke I had these tests Friday I should be studying for and a stupid oral report I haven't started.

Then he swept his shaky arm over the Scrabble board, ruining the game. Not that I was winning or anything, but still. He goes, "You need to start studying right now." When I told him I didn't even have my books with me, he insisted on helping me with my oral report.

Turns out he's got a whole bookshelf of poetry books, plus overflow stashed in his closet. We went through them, weeding out anything too girly, hard, old, or weird. Which got rid of most of them. We finally settled on something by Robert Frost.

After he helped me with the report, he made me go home and promise to study for Friday's tests. I really was going to. Until I turned the TV on just while I ate some Twinkies for energy, and saw *Patriot Games* just starting.

Wednesday, November 3

Dad called. Luckily I didn't answer the phone. Mom did. She spoke to him for 52 minutes, real quietly. I wonder what they talked about. Probably me. I wish I could have heard it. Then *Amanda* got on the phone. Only for 6 minutes, but for her a big deal. I'm supposed to call him back. Ugh.

Thursday, November 4

WHO WOULD BE GREAT TO HAVE AS A FATHER

1. Tony Gwynn. Great seats to Padres games, and he's supposed to be a really nice guy. (But then I'd be black. Hard to picture. Though I have the hair for it.)
2. George W. Bush. Secret Service guys would protect me from jocks attempting wedgies. (But I couldn't fantasize about Bush's wild twin girls anymore, they being my sisters.)
3. Bill Gates. Great computer toys, plus the inheritance.
4. Hugh Hefner. Playboy Bunnies running around the mansion.

5. Tom Cruise. Could borrow his race cars. But he'd probably be all over Gina. Never mind.

Friday, November 5

Went to the new slasher movie with Nate. He joked with these 8th graders in front of us all through the previews. During the first murder, he tickled the Asian girl on the back of her neck. He even got her phone number afterward.

I, on the other hand, just laughed at Nate's jokes like a talk show sidekick and tried to think of something to say. I bet he never would have introduced himself that day at lunch if he'd known I was such a shrub.

Maybe not a total shrub. After Spanish class today, Sydney said I had a beautiful accent. She goes, "I love how you roll your R's." Score one for Captain Sensitive.

I wish I'd said something besides thanks. Like that I was good with my tongue. She probably would have slapped me.

Nate wants to lose his virginity by the time he turns 16. I think I'll stick to my goal of 19. I'll be grateful just to kiss a girl by then.

Saturday, November 6

I'm too busy to deal with Dad. I have that stupid poetry report Monday. Besides, I'm a wimp. Got up early to call him during his 9:00 tennis match. Thank God for answering machines. "Hi, Dad, it's Mike. I won't be able to see you tomorrow. Bye."

Sunday, November 7

Amanda finally apologized about reading this journal. Now I only have 100 things to worry about, instead of 101.

It all started by Amanda coming into my room without knocking. I was sitting on the bed with her June *Cosmopolitan* that I snuck out of the trash last summer. Turned to page 67 as usual, that redhead in the $118 turquoise bikini. Who would pay that much for a bathing suit anyway? I slid the magazine under my pillow when she came in. I hope she didn't notice. She didn't say anything about it. But so what, she never said anything about my journal all this time.

She goes, "I think you should talk to Dad." Miss Superior! She doesn't talk to him for over a year, but she tells me to. I told her, "You butt into my room, you butt into my problems with Dad, and you butted into my journal." She says, "I didn't butt in about Dad. You were the one who called me last Sunday." Which is technically right.

I go, "What about my journal? You sure butted into that." She's like, "What?" Her face got all pink and she looked up at the ceiling. I should give her lying lessons, she's so pathetic at it. So I said, "That stuff you told Dad you could only know from reading my journal."

And then she did a half-assed apology. She said she could barely help it. She said I'm so quiet she never knows what's going on with me. Like it's my fault she read my journal.

Still, I sort of relate. Though I wouldn't tell Amanda

that. If she had a journal, I bet I'd be all over it. Hey, maybe she does have one. I should search her room.

We ended up having a big heart-to-heart. Totally cheesy. It's embarrassing how much I liked it.

Amanda's pretty smart, I guess. First of all, she explained that Gina's being pressured to have sex. Now that I think about it, it's obvious. The Incredible Hunk must always be trying to devirginize her. Then I had to make that joke and try to rush her in Scrabble and that's why Gina freaked out.

Hunk's such a jerk. She's only 14. I hope she doesn't give in. He's so hulky and hairy. He'd probably crush her. She'd probably never want to have sex again. It's too sick. I can't even think about it.

Amanda also tried to convince me how bad it is being popular. How everyone's really phony and all people talk about are looks and clothes and being popular. If it's so bad, then why does everyone want to be popular? You never see the A-list people asking if they can eat at the nerd table, or sitting by themselves at lunch. It is an option.

She even tried to complain about being pretty, how people don't appreciate anything else about you. I sort of get it, but on the other hand, I'm dorky-looking and people still don't appreciate anything about me. Amanda gave good advice about Gina, but if she thinks I'm all happy now about being unpopular and funny looking, she's definitely wrong.

She also listened to my report 4 times and gave me lots of tips. Since I know she can't read my journal anymore, I can write that it's good to have her around sometimes.

Monday, November 8

I'm so psyched! My poetry report went really well. Ms. Dore said I had an ear for poetry. Awesome. Sydney Holland told me she heard I did a great job. And she's not even in my English class. Maybe I've just got the Captain Sensitive rep now. It beats being called Storky.

I'm glad Duke helped me find a short poem without all that old English. Good old Robert Frost, "The Road Not Taken." Mark Gillespi did a Shakespeare sonnet with all these *thous* and *thines*, and I had no clue what he was talking about.

Nate went up right after me and totally choked. First he said his poem so quietly that Ms. Dore made him stop and do it over louder. The second time he talked a little louder, but started shaking. Even his voice shook. Painful. When he finished, the whole class was still, like everyone was embarrassed. Then I really felt sorry for him.

He left class as soon as the bell rang. I don't know where he went. I was so fired up at lunchtime I raced over to Amanda on the senior lawn. This is how wacked school is: if you touch the lawn and you're not a senior, they throw you in the Dumpster. So I had to stand on the concrete, shouting to Amanda like a squid.

She comes by with her best friend, Bulimic Michele, and I tell her I aced the report. I just wanted to thank her for her help. She gave me this look that could chill a polar bear, and goes, "I thought it was an emergency the way you geeked out." The whole time, Bulimic Michele won't even glance in my direction. Then they rush back to the popular people Amanda says she doesn't like, as if they're worried I could give them some disease. Dorkitis. It's like there's Home Amanda, who's nice, and School Amanda, who wishes we weren't related.

Whatever. Her little brother was a star today.

Tuesday, November 9

Finally talked to Dad today. He started off the phone call saying, "I don't understand what got into you last week." The guy makes big bucks managing all this technical engineering stuff at Qualcomm, but he pretends not to know why his son ran away from him.

Ordinarily I'd probably apologize for leaving the movie theater. Not tonight though. Maybe it was from acing the poetry report, or just being so mad at him. Whatever it was, I didn't back off. I told him I didn't like having to see his girlfriend every week.

Then Dad said, "She's quite fond of you." Quite fond of me. Yeah, right. That she's this important part of his life, that he loves her, blah blah blah. Instead of listening to me he had to defend himself. And I know The Thighmaster can't stand me. Saying she's quite fond of me is a big fat lie, and how stupid is Dad for trying to pull that over on me?

Not stupid. Just, I don't know, someone who thinks his son is stupid. But I'm not. Just ask my English teacher or Sydney Holland. I'm Captain Sensitive.

Then he got another call and put me on hold.

So I walked around my room with the cordless, thinking, I hate arguing with people, especially Dad. Thinking I should just see how things turn out Sunday—maybe The Thighmaster will be nicer. I waited forever. Well, 4½ minutes. I was ready to give in, like I usually do.

Then I started whispering my poem. I pictured myself in front of the Honors English class again, Gina staring at me with her big dark eyes, Ms. Dore scribbling notes. I remembered Duke going through all those old poetry books with me. And I imagined Robert Frost, hunched over a little wooden desk like mine, but without the computer and Princess Leia mousepad, writing out the poem with a long quill pen. I pictured myself telling my classmates that the road less traveled can make all the difference.

And then I imagined myself squishing my long Gumby body into the backseat of Dad's car, while The Thighmaster rode shotgun with her fake little smile.

That's when the poem clicked. I figured out what Frost was saying before, but tonight I really felt it. It was so weird, I almost saw a lightbulb turn on in front of me, like in those old Warner Brothers cartoons.

I thought about the usual road I take, just going along with people, waiting for things to happen. Waiting for Dad to get back on the phone. Waiting to see how it would go on Sunday. I decided right then to take a different road.

He got back on, not even apologizing for keeping me on hold so long, just saying, "Hi, Champ," like calling me Champ would make everything all right.

Then I said it: "I won't see you with your girlfriend."

Long silence. Then he goes, "Mike?" And I go, "Yeah?" He didn't say anything. Then I said, "Dad?" And he said, "What?" Then another silence. Then he finally goes, "I'll call you back," and he hung up on me.

So today I took a road less traveled. I don't even know what's going to happen with me and Dad now. But I'm 14 years old. I told him what I want. And that has made all the difference. I hope.

Wednesday, November 10

Heather Kvaas slid a note into Nate's locker today. I think I remember what it said exactly. I should. We stared at it long enough.

Your poetry reading sucked a lot.

But I still think you're pretty hot.

Have a great day.

Love, Heather K.

So I ace the report and get an A from Ms. Dore. Nate blows the report and gets a love note from one of the prettiest girls in 9th grade. Figures.

Thursday, November 11

Went to Golden Village today to thank Duke for giving me the poem. He wanted to show me more poems. Thought I might enjoy them. I'm not *that* much of a nerd. Though Duke said that when he was in high school, Shakespeare's sonnets and half a bottle of wine helped him score the first time. Cool.

I said I wanted to impress Gina with my sensitivity. I go, "She's in my class so she got to hear my report. Maybe I blew her away." Duke told me to take the road not taken, to ask her out. When I told him she's dating this dumb 11th grade jock, he just put his shaky hand on my shoulder and said, "She doesn't care about sensitive."

Friday, November 12

Gina looked so beautiful today. She was the 5th girl to do a Sylvia Plath poem, but hers was the best. She wore this long skirt with birds on it and a soft pink sweater and a little braid in her hair. I'm crazy about her. I didn't really get the poem though. Something about a dead Nazi.

All the girls talked about how Sylvia Plath died by putting her head in the oven. I don't understand that either. How could she have kept her head in there? Wouldn't you pull it out at the last minute? Did she get burned to death, or was there like a breathing problem? Why didn't she pick an easier way to go, for instance a quick bullet through the head or at least an overdose of Valium?

Saturday, November 13

Called Gina this morning to congratulate her on her poetry report. Wanted to tell her how pretty she looked in the pink sweater, but instead said, "You sound really knowledgeable about poetic structure." Lame.

I was hoping she'd say something about my poem. Like what a sensitive guy I must be. So sensitive she just knew I'd be a good boyfriend or at least boyfriend material. All she said was, "Why did Nate choke so bad on his report?"

I don't know. I never would have suspected. Not from a guy ballsy enough to show me his dirty playing cards that day in the crapeteria when he didn't know anything about me. And he doesn't seem to have a problem picking up girls.

I tried to answer Gina in a sensitive way. I actually said, "Poetry may be daunting to some people." Daunting. The vocab of Captain Sensitive.

But she interrupted me with an important announcement about the Incredible Hunk. He asked her to the Snowball. Supposedly, he's really sweet because the Snowball is more than a month away. And his face looked really sweet when he invited her. And he gave her this sweet kiss when she said yes. I bet he already rented a motel room.

Sunday, November 14

Dad took me to see the new James Bond flick. Just me and him. In a TV movie, we'd be all huggy and apologetic and form a deep father-son connection. But we just pretended like the whole fight never happened.

It was one of the quietest nights of my life. We have absolutely nothing to say to each other. It was so pathetic I even started missing The Thighmaster.

I need to figure out how to get Dad to like me. The only idea I can think of is joining a sports team. Something real macho. Obviously I'm not cut out for wrestling. And it's too late for football this year, thank God. I could try basketball.

Wait, I hate basketball. I mean, I love watching basketball on TV or whatever and reading about it in the newspaper. But I hate actually playing basketball. I hate playing any sports. Except bowling and channel surfing.

What's better? Staying after school most days aiming balls into a basket while you sweat like a pig and people jab you with their elbows? Or sitting in a car with someone in total silence who's your own dad but can't stand you?

At least when he teaches me to drive, we'll have something to talk about.

Monday, November 15

Tonight started off weird right from the beginning. Dr. Vermin called, and I said, "My mom's watering the backyard," and he goes, "I wanted to speak to you, Mike." I'm thinking, Why did I have to answer the phone? I was so happy on the couch with my Fritos, watching the aliens from Planet Genius on *Jeopardy*.

He was at the bowling alley. It was so noisy I could barely hear him. He wanted me to bowl. One of the guys on his team broke his thumb, and they'd have to forfeit if they couldn't get someone. He told me there are all these teenagers in the league, lots of fathers and sons. I said, "I'm not your son." And he goes, "I know."

I asked him if there were any girls in the league. Then he did that isn't-he-cute laugh that totally bugs. He's like, "No, but there's 4 pretty teenage girls a couple lanes over from us."

He kept begging, so I figured maybe I can get something

out of this. I said, "I might bowl if you'll buy me some nachos." He goes, "You're on, John," which he must think is current teen slang. Pathetic. Then he started begging again. Just to shut him up, I guess, I said I'd do it.

Mom practically did cartwheels when I asked her to drive me. Like telling Dr. Vermin I'd bowl has anything to do with liking him. It was just to get him off my back, maybe take a look at those 4 girls, and because I hadn't bowled since I got that 205. It's hard to find people to bowl with.

So Dr. Vermin was pretty cool, for a guy who's screwing my mom. Except he lied about teenage girls bowling nearby. At least he admitted he lied. And I can understand why he did it. He was pretty desperate for a substitute. He didn't mention Mom at all the whole time. That was nice of him. I bowled a 158, a 167, and a 189. Decent.

He wants me to call him Howard, but I don't know. You use first names for adults you see a lot of. I'm not planning on hanging with him or anything. This was a one-shot thing. Plus it's a horrible name. Just saying Howard out loud could make me even more of a nerd.

Tuesday, November 16

Nate told me he choked on the English report on purpose so Ms. Dore would feel sorry for him and give him a decent grade. Uh huh.

I'm not really mad at him for that lame lie. It's hard to be pissed off at someone when you feel sorry for him. I should be a lawyer when I grow up. I always see both sides of everything. I can't see Mom as a lawyer though. She's not oily enough. I'd be oily enough.

At first I was going to let it go. Then, thinking about that poem, the new road I'm taking now, I told Nate, "I don't like being lied to. You lied to me about your house too, how you had all those TVs and a den, and it doesn't have that at all."

Then he started psychologizing. He said his life is so crappy, he has to make up stuff about it. He told me how his dad doesn't give his mom any money and only sees him every year or so.

His dad moved to Reno a long time ago, and just shows up at Nate's house with presents that are always wrong. Like last year he got him a down coat. Hello, we live in San Diego. Once he brought over a puppy and Nate's mom put it right back in his car. The D.A.'s office is helping his mom sue for child support, but Nate says any money his dad ever had is at the blackjack tables in Reno. Compared to Nate's dad, mine is Father of the Year.

Wednesday, November 17

Had the house to myself for 2 hours tonight. I don't think Amanda keeps a diary. But she does have 3 condoms, *The Joy of Sex* with Post-its, love notes from 6 different guys plus someone named Elizabeth, and a picture of herself and Dad at her middle school graduation. I guess I'm the only virgin in this house.

I wonder what Gina writes in her diary. Is my name mentioned even once? With my luck every page of the journal I gave her is filled with love poems to Hunk. I can just imagine: He caught a pass for our great school. His pecs and ass are really cool. She probably taped his picture on the cover and kisses it every night before she starts writing. I'm making myself sick.

Thursday, November 18

STORY OF A TOTAL LOSER

1. He bikes to his friend's house after school. She thinks he's a friend, but he can't get it through his fat head that's all they are.

2. It starts raining on the way over. He's not wearing a jacket. His Brillo pad hair instantly turns into a Jewfro.

3. In his backpack is a thin gold necklace with a small *G* charm, a birthday present that took 4 hours to pick out and that he spent 31 minutes wrapping the night before. A card taped to the present took 23 minutes to choose as the mall was closing, while the saleslady at Suzy's Hallmark shot him dirty looks and flicked the lights on and off. The card has a message handwritten on it that took him 37 minutes to compose last night. "Happy birthday to the nicest 15-year-old in the universe. I hope I get to see you for all your birthdays. Sincerely, Mike." He laid

awake for 86 minutes wondering if the message was too corny. Total time spent on said birthday present: 6 hours and 57 minutes.

4. When he gets to her house, he takes the present out of the backpack. It is wet and the bow is smooshed. The word Gina on the card's envelope is runny.

5. He rings the doorbell.

6. Gina answers the door with one hand. Her other hand is holding Hunk's. She is wearing a necklace like the one he bought for her, only the chain is thicker and the *G* is bigger.

7. He runs to his bike while stuffing the present in his backpack.

8. He pedals quickly.

9. He falls going down Gina's driveway.

10. He hears Gina say, "Mike, are you okay?" and Hunk shout, "Need a hand, Storky?"

11. He gets back up, doesn't turn around, and bikes home. His face is all wet. He tells himself it's from the rain.

Fry Ember 19

Me and Nate go movies. Snuck bottle of win. I so bum thinking bout Gina and Inedible Hunk. Threw up gain. Into popcorn tub. Lucky jumbo size. 2 time. Maybe 3. Maybe 3. I go sleep now. Still fell little out of it. I hop I make sense. Luck I spill check.

Saturday, November 20

Mom took away the TV for the whole rest of the year. Where does she hide that thing? I woke up this morning and it was gone. Mom gave me this big talk and all these threats about drinking, but I had trouble concentrating. My head was pounding so much, I just sat on the flowery couch like a rock, trying not to move.

After the lecture I called Nate. He said I was slurring my words, and then I fell asleep in Mom's car after the movie with my mouth open like a candy bowl. Nate said after I passed out, she started going off on him. She yelled at him for being a Bad Influence and kept calling him Mister and Young Man. I don't even remember the drive home.

Monday, November 22

Gina came over to copy my English notes. She didn't mention Hunk all night. She did this whole thing about a hypothetical girl who has a hypothetical crush on a hypothetical guy who thinks he's just her friend. She goes, "Hypothetically speaking, what should the girl do about it?"

The whole time she talked I thought, There is a God, my prayers have been answered. I stared at her little glossy lips, wanting to kiss them. Except I was also thinking I had that chili cheese dog with onions for lunch, and even Nate said my breath should come with a poison warning.

I go, trying to sound calm, "Anyone I know?" She got all embarrassed. Then she said, "It's Heather Kvaas." Not a total bummer at that point, since Heather's so pretty and all. I tried to remember any clues that Heather liked me. Then Gina says, "Don't tell Nate, but Heather has a crush on him." And I said, "Oh."

Nate's got it so good. Except for his flaky dad, and chain-smoking mom, and crummy little house, and bombing the poetry reading. Never mind.

Tuesday, November 23

At lunch today, Nate walked over to Heather's table in the crapeteria, took her aside, and asked her to the Snowball. He's so cool with girls. I would have written down what I wanted to say, practiced it a zillion times in front of the mirror, put it off a week, and then wimped out at the last minute.

Nate wants me to double-date with them, but I don't think I have it in me. Gina's going with Hunk, of course. I could ask Sydney Holland. Nate gives it 4 to 1 odds she'd say yes. He says she stares at my back in Spanish class with this spacy expression on her face. Plus she always seems to be right by my locker, like more than a coincidence. I'm probably hallucinating. Anyway, I can't dance and I don't want to watch Gina and the Hunk make out.

Maybe I could learn to dance, and maybe Sydney would kiss me, and she'd have her braces off by then so it wouldn't hurt my tongue or anything, and maybe Gina would get jealous, and realize I was her true love. So I should just ask her because it could be the best night of my life.

Wednesday, November 24

Aye caramba! Mierda! Que un baboso! Today's journal entry will be deleted about 5 seconds after I print it.

I bet this whole thing never would have happened if my Spanish teacher had shown up today, or if the sub had worn a skirt instead of those tight pants.

That sub had the biggest lips I ever saw. Huge puffy ones, like two Costco hot dogs resting on her face. Maybe if she hadn't worn those tight polyester pants, I wouldn't have wondered what she could do with those lips.

No. I'm such a perv I would have thought about it if she was wearing a potato sack. Come to think of it, during the potato sack race at the school picnic last spring, I kept picturing me and Gina making out in one of the sacks.

Besides the usual sex stuff, I wondered if those big lips gave the sub a special talent for horn instruments or if she could blow up balloons really fast. But I kept getting back to the pervy stuff.

Probably it wouldn't have happened if Hot Lips hadn't called me up to the board to conjugate *estar*. It's so easy. *Estoy, estas, esta, estamos, estan.* I walked up there just fine. Maybe it was the way she put the marker in my hand, touching my palm a little, sexy-like.

I got a boner at the whiteboard. It was those big lips. There he stood, Rex, king of kings, trying to pop out of my Levi's.

I kept my back to the class, whispering, "Chill, Rex, chill, Rex" and staring at the board. I tried to picture David Spade naked, and Whoopi Goldberg on the can, but Rex wouldn't come down. It didn't help when Hot Lips went, "Are you having a hard time?" Very hard.

I thought if I could stall long enough, Rex could come down before I had to turn around. I wrote *estoy* really slowly. Then Hot Lips said, "What's up?" Rex was up. I just stood at the whiteboard, staring at it, pretending to think about the next word.

This has to be the most humiliating day of my life. Why do these things always happen to me? I'm getting embarrassed just typing this.

Like things weren't bad enough, Hot Lips asked who'd like to give me a hand. Sydney Holland must have sprinted out of her seat. Just thinking about Sydney's hand made Rex even happier. I didn't need a hand. I needed a tranquilizer dart. She got to about an inch from me, looked down at Rex, and whispered, "Oh my God, Mike."

"What's the big deal?" Hot Lips asked. Which made Sydney laugh. I managed to write *estas*. Sydney picked up a marker, but she shook so bad, she couldn't even write. She has this silent laugh, like Gina's. I saw her smile and nod her head up and down, but no noise came out. Hot Lips goes, "What is so hard here?," which caused Sydney to double over.

I tried to remember what Dr. Berman's fat butt looked like while he was bowling, but Rex stayed airborne. I hate being a guy sometimes. Girls never have this problem. I guess their nipples can get pointy, but it's not the same.

After I wrote *estamos*, I pictured that thing on Discovery I saw last week. They showed this beautiful forest, and zoomed in closer and closer, to a snowy clearing, and then to this brown furry dead animal lying on its back. Finally they closed in on the thing's face and all these huge white maggots just ripping into it. Skeazy. As I remembered it, Rex finally calmed down. I finished *estan*.

By that time, Sydney had staggered to her seat doing her silent laugh while Hot Lips told her to get a grip. I forced myself not to think about Sydney's grip.

Sydney stood near my locker today after school, but I pretended to be in a big hurry to get home. I'm not asking her to the Snowball or anywhere else.

Thursday, November 25

So tired. I laid awake most of last night stressing over the Rex Incident. For all I know, Sydney wrote up the whole story for the school paper or broadcast it all over the Internet. I was half expecting to find Rex's picture in the San Diego newspaper today, with the headline Local Boy Finds High School Exciting.

I'm also tired from eating so much. Mom ordered a big Thanksgiving dinner from Albertsons and invited all these people over, and I pigged out. Albertsons sure is better than Mom's cooking. Duke was supposed to come, but he has strep throat. If I was a decent human being, I'd go visit him.

MY IMPRESSIONS OF THE PEOPLE THERE
1. *Dr. Vermin.* Minus 2. Tried to take over my job of cutting the turkey. I can just see him moving in.

2. *Mom*. Plus 5. Nice of her to invite Nate and his mom, the walking ashtray. Great idea not to try cooking again—especially after last year's pink turkey disaster.

3. *Aunt Marsha*. Minus 1. Pretty pathetic. You could tell she was missing June the whole time. Wish she'd meet a nice lesbian lady. I wonder where they find each other anyway.

4. *Nate*. Plus 6. Denied hearing any rumors about me and Spanish class. He goes, "Anyway, I know more about you than some gossiphead." He also deserves points for putting up with his mom.

5. *Nate's mom*. Minus 6. Half the night she stood in the backyard puffing away on her cancer sticks. The other half she chugged red wine. I bet she drank a whole bottle.

6. *Grandma*. Minus 8. Spent the night insulting people, especially Mom. Said the kitchen counter needed re-grouting, called my table manners primitive. Told Mom she'd be better off in cooking school than law school. Actually made me feel sorry for Mom.

7. *Amanda*. Plus 3. Did this phony toast to Mom. Said she's this great role model for going to law school and hosting Grandma and everyone right before her finals.

I wonder what it's like at Golden Village tonight. I hope they served turkey. And a Jell-O mold thing for those dentally challenged.

I hope Duke's okay.

Friday, November 26

THINGS TO DO WITHOUT A TV

1. Read a book.
2. Visit Duke.
3. Memorize Scrabble words.
4. Lift weights.
5. Stare at Victoria's Secret catalog again.
6. Watch TV at Nate's.
7. Bike to Circuit City and watch TV there.

Sunday, November 28

Saw Dad without his bimbo delight tonight. The Thigh-master wants him to lose 10 pounds. She's got him on this diet. Dad has a little tire belly, but it's not like he's fat. Since The Thighmaster wasn't there tonight, me and Dad went to Burger King and each ordered a Double Whopper, fries, onion rings, and a chocolate shake. Sure beats the rabbit food restaurants he's been taking me to lately.

He seemed so happy to eat normal food, I got up my nerve to ask him the question. "Dad. Once I turn 15 and get my permit, will you teach me to drive?" He said, "No problem." Yes!

I even thought about telling him stuff like my crush on Gina, and my poetry report, and the Rex Incident. But, I don't know. It seemed like too much work. I wasn't sure where to start, or how, or why. Plus he didn't really ask.

I wish I had something good to say. Like, Hey, Dad, right after I scored the winning soccer goal at the home game, 2 cheerleaders asked me to the Snowball simultaneously. That he'd be interested in.

We mostly just talked about the food and football.

Monday, November 29

I hope Sydney Holland keeps her mouth shut about the Rex Incident. She stood by my locker after school, twirling her frizzy hair. I gave her this mini-wave, to let her know I saw her but wasn't exactly thrilled.

Luckily I had Nate with me. We were going to bike to his house. He had leftover sausage pizza, plus the TV.

When Nate and I walked off, she rushed after us, going, "I really want to talk to you, Mike." At least she didn't call me Storky. Or something worse, like Stiffy or Woody. I said, "We're in a hurry," as if the pizza would explode if we didn't get there in precisely 9 minutes. And she goes, "I just need to speak to you about something private." Nate offered to wait by the locker, but I went, "No, no, we have to go." And I rushed off.

When Nate caught up to me, he asked, "Why did you blow her off? She's so into you." I didn't say anything. Nate said my face was red. He goes, "I bet you like her, but you're too scared." I didn't tell him she saw me with a boner and I think she wants to blackmail me.

What a mess. I'll deny everything. I'll say, What was

Sydney Holland doing staring at my crotch? I'll say my johnson's so big it just looked like it was hard. Oh, man, she better not tell anyone.

Wednesday, December 1

I'm never seeing Duke again. And it's not because he scored 403 points in Scrabble and did a victory lap in his wheelchair with the old geezers cheering him on. Even though that totally bugged.

On his way back from the victory lap, he goes, "Don't be glum, son. If I can stay alive another decade, you might win a game." Hahaha. What a laugh riot. I told him, "Lucky you, I'm not your son." It was supposed to be a joke, I guess, but it didn't come out that way. More like pathetic.

He got all serious and grabbed my hand in his wrinkly one, which was even worse than Berman's hand in my hair. He goes, "Your parents should consider themselves quite fortunate. I know your mother does."

I wanted to say, Spare me. And my hand. Sure, the 1 percent of my time I spend at Golden Village, Mom beams like a flashlight. But the other 99 percent of my time, when I didn't visit you when you were sick, or when I'm watching TV or inhaling the refrigerator or holed up in the bathroom with that Natalie Portman picture Nate got off the Internet, Mom isn't high-fiving herself on what a great son she raised.

I told Duke, "Mom likes everyone. Even that hard-ass nurse you say reminds you of Kathy Bates in *Misery*. Mom said she just went into the wrong profession."

Then he tightened his pruny hand around mine and goes, "It's your father, isn't it? You think you haven't earned his respect. He deserves better than you, right?"

Where did he get that anyway? From Mom? Was she psychoanalyzing me behind my back? Or maybe he just knew I'm too geeky a kid for a dad to be proud of.

It doesn't matter how he knew, because I'm never seeing him again. I don't need his crap. I have more than enough adults in my life. Mom. Dad. The Thighmaster. Berm. I don't need to bike to a nursing home to get harassed about my dad not liking me.

I pulled my hand out and said, "I'm just here for the Scrabble tips." Then I left so fast, I didn't even look at him. I hope Duke's face got as glum as he always said mine was.

Thursday, December 2

Just finished the greatest book in the world. Berm gave it to me. *Catcher in the Rye*. It's about this teenage guy who's really smart and doesn't fit in at school. He goes off on his own one weekend and meets all these phonies and keeps saying *goddamn* and then goes crazy.

Like the whole time I read it, I went, Yeah, that's right, so true. He had so many observations that I always think about in the back of my mind. He got put in the nuthouse, but it was like the whole universe was off and he was the only sane one.

I'm not telling Berman how much I liked it. He'll get all proud of himself for giving it to me.

Saturday, December 4

Totally awesome night! I'm so psyched I can't sleep. I rescued Gina. I'm going on a date with her. I'm like her hero now maybe. Gina might even be writing about me in her journal right now.

It all started when I was sitting on my bed leafing through my old comic books. That's how bored I was. Amanda and Mom were both out—not together, of course. So when the phone rang, I picked up. I'm so glad I did.

As soon as I said hello, I heard Gina crying on the other end. She said "Mike," or more like sobbed it, like a 4-syllable name. Mi-i-i-ike.

I go, "What's wrong?" and then I just heard her gulping. Every time she tried to talk, she kept crying or gulping. Finally, she got out that she'd had this fight with Hunk, and she'd walked by herself in the dark from his house to Denny's, and she was calling me from the pay phone, and she didn't want to tell her parents, and she didn't know what to do.

So I said, "Wait right there, I'll get you." Like I could drive. Or owned a car. Or knew when Amanda would be home.

After I hung up, I laid on my bed totally blanking out, going, What did I just say? But I couldn't let Gina down. I felt sorry for her, but also it was my big chance to be Captain Sensitive, especially with Hunk acting like such a jerk.

So I thought, Taxi, and leapt out of bed and started searching for money. I had $16.25 in my wallet. I grabbed the $2 bill and the Susan B. Anthony dollar I was saving too. I didn't know if that was enough. It's not like I take taxis every day. Then I remembered all that change in the junk drawer, so while I waited for the cab, I went through the junk and dug up another $4.13.

The taxi driver didn't say anything on the way there except, "Vas di address?" He had this really thick accent.

Gina looked so sweet in the Denny's booth, her makeup all smeared under her dark eyes and a big stain on her blouse. I think it was coffee.

I gave her a hug, and she hugged me back, real long. I should have been psyched, I guess, but I kept thinking how the taxi meter was running and I only had $23.38, which was supposed to be for Christmas and Hanukkah gifts. Plus, Gina said, "I couldn't think who'd be home on a Saturday night besides you."

Gina gave me the details in the cab. How Hunk got all pissed that she wouldn't sleep with him, and called her names. She said if she told me the names, she'd burst into tears. What a jerk. How Hunk said he was sick of waiting. And he wasn't taking her to the Snowball since he'd be the only junior at our school who didn't get laid after the dance. Then Gina said she and Heather had just bought semiformal dresses today at Charlotte Russe, but it came out Ru-u-u-usse, because she was crying again.

I gave her another hug. Then the cabdriver goes in his accent, "He take you to dance. Let boy take you."

That bugged. First of all, I'm supposed to be a man, not a boy. Second of all, how'd he know I wasn't already going?

Could he tell I was a loser that fast? Third of all, why didn't I think of asking her first?

I said, "Sure I'll take you," trying to act like I was doing her a huge favor. Like it was nothing, though I could hardly get the words out. Gina goes, "Really?" I nodded, but I guess she didn't see me. Then I said yes, but my voice cracked, so I said *yes* again real loud. Then *she* thanked *me*, and I said, "My pleasure," trying to sound macho. But it came out all soft and she said, "What?" And the cabdriver goes, "He say my pleasures."

I should have tipped him more than $2. But after shelling out the $19.50 fare, I was pretty broke.

After I walked Gina to her door, she kissed me. On the lips. Just a short little nip. Not a big sexy one like in the movies, but it felt excellent.

When I got in, Mom smelled my breath and checked my eyes in the light. It's like she's my probation officer now. Who cares anyway, I'm going to the Snowball! With Gina! Awesome!

Sunday, December 5

Dad couldn't see me tonight. He's eating brown rice and getting massages at some spa in Palm Springs.

Fine. Because I need to do a lot of planning for the Snowball anyway. First, how are we supposed to get there? Have Mom drive with that isn't-my-little-boy-cute look the whole way there? We could double-date with Nate and Heather, but what if they're making out the whole time and we aren't? Or what if Heather and Gina hang together all night and leave me and Nate in the dust?

Also, what about clothes? My suit's from the bar mitzvah circuit era. I doubt it still fits. And I have to buy Gina a corsage and dinner probably too. Where can I get the money? I spent what I had on the taxi. Mom will probably fork some over, since she likes Gina so much. Better be nice to Mom the next 13 days.

Oh, man, I just thought of this: What if Hunk finds out I'm taking Gina to the Snowball and beats the crap out of me? Maybe Gina would feel sorry for me and kiss me and I'd be her hero. A hero for getting the crap beaten out of him?

And I just remembered something else. I can't dance. What am I going to do the next 13 days? I'm already going nuts.

Monday, December 6

Bowled a 184 tonight. Since I still have 26 boring days until I get the TV back and Berm said he'd buy me all the junk food I could cram into my mouth, I joined the team. As soon as their old teammate's thumb heals, they'll probably kick me off.

The league is through Berm's temple. He goes to the big reform one in La Jolla. I always wanted to be in a reform temple. You can get bar mitzvahed without learning much Hebrew. And since a lot of the prayers are in English, you can understand what they're saying. Cubby Horowitz's bar mitzvah service at that temple was only 84 minutes long.

When I made the bar mitzvah circuit, I always sat in the back and snuck a word search into the prayer book. If there is a God, and You either saw what I did or You're reading my journal, I hope You're not pissed off. Actually, I hope You have better things to do with Your time. Like cure AIDS or something.

I didn't think you could find enough Jews to bowl. I could understand if it was a Chinese restaurant club or a Jewish lawyers club. Berm said his temple even has a camping club. I bet they all use motor homes.

The other guys on our team are this bald guy Lester and his son Dan. I see where Berman got the hair-ruffling idea. Lester's always doing it to Dan. Maybe because he has no hair of his own to mess with. I hope I never go bald. Not that having a Brillo pad on your head is so great, but it's better than nothing. Lester's always praising Dan. Even when he got a gutter ball tonight, Lester goes, "Nice try." Dan just looked at me and rolled his eyes. You can tell Lester thinks he's the greatest father in the world. Having that weekly bonding thing with Dan, and spouting off his barfulous lines about sportsmanship and teamwork and junk. At least Berm just jokes around and bowls and gives high fives every so often. Of course, he's not my father.

Wednesday, December 8

I can't believe how popular I am. Things are picking up for this old nerd. When Sydney came by our lunch table, I thought for sure it was to bring up the Rex Incident. I was all set to argue with her. Or beg.

Then she asked me to the Snowball. She stammered it, like I was important. When I told her I already had a date, I think I saw tears in her eyes. Nate's been calling me Babe Magnet all afternoon.

Wish I could tell Duke about Gina and Sydney. Why did I have to be so jerky to him last time? I bet he's still mad. I can't go over there. He'd probably get all his geezer friends to ream me with their canes.

Thursday, December 9

I can't trust anyone. If I wait long enough, they all screw me. Amanda read my journal, Nate lied, Dad doesn't care, and now this.

Mom told me to stop messing up the house. That Dr. Vermin had the TV at his condo. After all the time I spent tearing everything apart searching for it. I knew Verm wasn't the Mr. Nice Guy he pretends to be.

Mom says it was her idea, but so what? Verm went along with it. She didn't even apologize. She said she knew I'd look all over the house for the TV. Like it's my fault her boyfriend took it. And what if they broke up? Verm would probably keep the TV and I'd never see it again.

I should go live with Aunt Marsha. She's probably so lonely it would cheer her up. I couldn't live with Dad. He wouldn't want me. I called him to see if he could pick me up early Sunday so we could go suit shopping, and all he said was that it's not a good plan. He didn't even ask what I needed the suit for.

On top of everything, I can't even yell at Mom too much because I need the money for the Snowball. We're double dating with Nate and Heather. His mom will drive both ways. I hope she doesn't smoke in the car. Maybe Nate can say something to her.

Mom was bummed when I turned down her offer to drive. Good. I hate her. And I hate her fat, lying boyfriend. And I hate Dad. And Amanda for hogging up all the popularity and looks genes in the family. And Osama bin Laden, of course. And the Chargers for choking all the time. And everyone else in the world. Except Gina. And Sydney. And I guess Nate's okay. And possibly Duke.

If I was still talking to Duke, I'd tell him I was right about Vermin being a jerk. And about Gina liking me. Duke had it all wrong. I think he did anyway.

Friday, December 10

Mom gave me $200 for Hanukkah. Excellent! She taped it under a package of new socks. The pathetic thing is that before I saw the money, I wasn't even fazed that Amanda got a CD player and all I got was socks.

Vermin came over with the TV. Said he didn't want to be in the middle of everything. He even apologized. Which is cool. Grownup-to-kid apology is a pretty rare thing. Mom put the TV in the garage and said if I sneak it, I'll lose it for another month.

Verm acts like he likes me. I wonder if he really does, or if he's just trying to get on Mom's good side. What if he's secretly planning to march me off to military school or torture me with his dental equipment?

Sunday, December 12

Dad wants to change our visits to every other week. Says he has a lot of work to do. Probably he's just tired of making excuses every other week for why he doesn't want to see me. I bet if Amanda came along, he'd be there every Sunday right on time.

Tonight Dad was even quieter than usual. Like he barely spoke. I knew something was wrong, so I asked how his girlfriend was doing. He goes, "We broke up." I said I was sorry. Sure I was.

When someone says, We broke up, that always means he got dumped. Otherwise he'd say, I broke up with her. Another one is, It didn't work out. That also means, I got dumped. Amanda told me that. She also said taking Gina to the Snowball is a violation of Cardinal Rule of Dating #6: Never date someone on the rebound. What does she know?

Dad gave me a Hanukkah present. He drove over to the ATM and takes out 5 twenties. He hands them to me and goes, "Here's a Hanukkah present so you can buy a suit."

When he did that, I thought about the latkes we used to

make. Before the Divorce. How we'd all cook latkes together the first night of Hanukkah. Dad would come home from work early and he'd wear that dorky apron Amanda made him in 7th grade. We'd use a huge bag of potatoes and some onions and take turns grating and frying, and everyone would pig out. It was just our family.

Mom tried to do it with me and Amanda a couple years ago, but Amanda said she was on a diet, and I started a grease fire, and Mom ended up yelling at us.

Dad never asked why I needed a suit. I didn't even mention the Snowball. Like he'd be interested. I sure didn't tell him Mom already gave me money. Maybe I can buy some decent computer games now. Or I could use it to take Gina out again. Only 6 more days until the Snowball.

I don't even care that Dad's cutting back on the visits. Well, not much, I guess. Was Duke really saying Dad deserved a better son than me? Not that I deserved a better dad, right? I'll never know now.

Wednesday, December 15

Haven't seen Sydney at my locker since she asked me to the Snowball. I miss her in a weird way. In Spanish class she stares somewhere else every time I turn to look at her.

Nate wants to go to Romero's on Saturday. It's right down the block from school, so we could walk to the dance from there. He found these 2-for-1 coupons. He says girls always go to the can after dinner because they have bean-sized bladders (lima? kidney? green bean?) and have to redo their makeup after any kind of movement like eating. So Nate can just slip out the coupon while they're in the john and they'll never know. I don't want Gina thinking I'm a cheapskate, but I bet we can pull it off. 3 more days until the Snowball.

Friday, December 17

I'm all set for the Snowball. I'm going to bed right after I write this entry, which will be short. I should be finished by 9:50, asleep by 10:00.

I sort of know how to dance now, I guess. Aunt Marsha says I'm a natural. She's probably just trying to build up my self-esteem. I don't think I totally suck. People won't be pointing and laughing. Anyway, it'll be dark in there.

Glad I got up the nerve to call Aunt Marsha and ask for help. I totally trust her. She swore she wouldn't tell anyone what we were up to.

Aunt Marsha taught me some cool dance moves. And it gave us both something to do on Friday night. Beats my usual routine of watching MTV and eavesdropping on Amanda's dates. Since June dumped her, I bet Aunt Marsha hasn't done much either.

It's now 9:48. I'm going to bed. I'll be completely rested for tomorrow.

Saturday, December 18

It's 12:09 and I've been lying awake for 2 hours and 19 minutes. What if Aunt Marsha taught me to dance like a lesbian? Maybe she goes to gay bars and the women have their own style and everyone at school will think I'm a lesbian. That doesn't make sense. Guys can't be lesbians. But what if she never goes dancing anymore and she taught me old dance steps that no one does now?

What if Hunk is at the dance and beats me up? Or what if Sydney's there and starts crying when she sees me with Gina? What if Sydney beats me up? She's pretty big, and she's on the swim team. She could probably take me.

I have to go to sleep. This is nuts.

Saturday, December 18

It's 1:32. My stomach is killing me. It's like someone's kneading dough in there. How old was that tofu-prune casserole Aunt Marsha gave me for dinner? That thing was barfulous. How can you tell if tofu goes bad? Maybe it's the prunes. With my luck I'll have the runs at the dance tonight.

Saturday, December 18

10 WORST THINGS ABOUT THE SNOWBALL IN HELL

1. My nonstop yawning.
2. The coupon ordeal.
3. Sydney Holland was there.
4. I didn't see the boob-flashing thing.
5. Nate got pissed at me.
6. Nate's mom morphed into Mike Wallace.
7. Amanda said, I told you so.

8. Gina.
9. Gina.
10. Gina.

ONLY GOOD THINGS ABOUT THE SNOWBALL
1. Nate's mom didn't smoke.
2. I didn't get beat up.
3. Sydney Holland was there.
4. Nate saw the boob-flashing thing and provided details.
5. It's over.

I can't write any more tonight of what was supposed to be like the best experience of my pitiful life. I'm too mad to try to sort it out. I'd probably start yelling. Or call Gina and yell at her.

Tonight I really am going to sleep. I wish I could just keep sleeping until I'm out of high school.

Sunday, December 19

Since yesterday was my first date and the worst night of my life, I'm forcing myself to write about it. If I ever want to blow a ton of money on a girl again, I'll look back at this entry and buy a bunch of computer games instead. In 20 years, when people ask why I never got married, I'll let them read this and they'll understand.

So here goes. The night started off fine. After Mom took a zillion pictures, she dropped me off at Nate's and we told each other how hot we looked. I got to sit in back with the girls on the way there. Nate already called the backseat for the trip home. He figured Heather might make out with him by then.

First we got Heather. She looked sexy. No bra. Just her body and this little thin black dress with no straps or sleeves or anything to hold up her boobs. Not that she has much.

Then we got Gina. She looked beautiful. She wore these little butterflies in her hair, barrettes, I guess, and a powder-blue dress with a long slit up her leg. All night I got to see flashes of her leg through the slit when she moved the right way. She gave me a hug at her door and I had to remember the last 10 American presidents to keep Rex in line.

Nate's mom didn't say anything the whole way there, which made her the ideal driver. The disasters started after she dropped us off at Romero's. All these people were waiting for a table. The hostess goes, "You have reservations?" Nate and I looked at each other. Nate whispers no, and she goes, "There's an hour wait unless you want to eat at the bar."

So my first dinner out with a girl, we sit on these high barstools where our feet can't even reach the floor. Real mature. Right next to me, this older lady, like Mom's age, was totally plastered. Her boyfriend or date or whatever he was kept asking her to go to his apartment, and she kept laughing at him like a mule and begging the bartender for one more drink. Sad.

Gina and I hardly talked to each other. It was too loud.

The food was decent, but I kept thinking I could have bought tickets to a Chargers game for what our chicken parmesans cost.

I stressed the whole time because the girls didn't go to the bathroom like Nate said they would, and we needed to give the waiter the coupon. Plus I didn't know whether to order dessert or not. I didn't want to look like a pig and be the only one eating, but I didn't want to look like a cheapskate either.

It turned out that no one ordered dessert. The waiter gave us the check, but the girls didn't make any kind of moves to go to the can. Finally, Nate just hid the coupon between our twenties and the bill.

The waiter picked out the coupon, held it up, and stared at it like it was a UFO. He got all attitudinal. He goes, "Present Coupon Upon Ordering. It says it right here. Now I have to recalculate the bill."

I caught Heather and Gina shaking their heads at each other. I bet the Incredible Hunk never uses coupons on a date. Even with the discount, the dinner set me back $37.50.

So after all that, the girls decided to go to the bathroom right as we were leaving. When they left, Nate told me he could see right into Heather's dress and he thought he even got a peek at her right nipple.

Oh, man, I typed all this and I didn't even get to the dance yet. I'll just say that we walked there and Nate held Heather's hand the whole way. She had him hold her purse too. Wish I had a picture of that. With her other hand she kept pulling up the top of her dress. Gina held her purse with the hand closest to mine, like letting me know *not* to take her hand.

The dance itself sucked because of Gina. It started to suck right away. As soon as we got in line at the auditorium, with the security guards checking everyone for weapons and drugs, we saw Hunk. He stood 2 people ahead of us. He had his arm around this really tall skinny girl. Actually it rested on her butt. She looked old—18, maybe—definitely older than Gina. When she turned around, I saw she wasn't that hot. Her face was too long, like that actress who played Phoebe on *Friends*.

Gina kept staring at them. It got to the point where Heather had to ask if she was okay. She nodded, but I knew right then that Amanda was right about Cardinal Rule of Dating #6. I shouldn't date a girl on the rebound, even Gina. To her I was just an escort, someone who bought the tickets so she could go to the Snowball and show off her butterflies and her new dress.

This is hard to write. I'm so totally bummed, my fingers feel all slow and heavy on the keyboard.

But I'll keep going, for the record. As soon as we got in, the girls headed for the bathroom again. Nate was too psyched about holding Heather's hand and seeing her right nipple to care about my problems with Gina. We stood at the refreshment table pigging out on the cookies.

When they left the ladies' room like 10 hours later, Gina's eyes were all red. She checked out the dance floor right away. Hunk and Phoebe from *Friends* were swaying together, total cling-ons. Before Heather would dance with Nate, she asked Gina, "You'll be all right?" Gina nodded, like if she said anything she'd start crying again.

I asked Gina to dance, but she turned me down. We sat on the folding chairs on the edge of the dance floor while she stared at Hunk. She didn't want punch. She didn't want to get our pictures taken, which was okay because that cost $15. She just wanted to watch Hunk and Phoebe from *Friends* and sigh and be depressed.

It seemed like everyone else was on the dance floor, all sweaty and smiley. Sydney too. She wore this lacy one-shouldered green dress that matched her eyes. She and her friend Miranda were spazzing out to "Who Let the Dogs Out," going "woof woof woof" and everything, but spazzing in a good way, like they didn't care about not having dates.

Sydney's legs looked fantastic. I guess her breasts always had me so distracted before that I never noticed her legs. I mean, really noticed them. Or maybe it was what she was wearing last night. A very short dress and black spiky shoes. She seriously could be a leg model. Is that a real job? I know there's bathing suit models and hand models. Sydney should check into leg modeling as a career. I'm getting off track again.

Miranda saw me first. She gave me the evil eye and then said something in Sydney's ear. Probably "Storky." When Sydney glanced at me, her eyes lit up bright green like she was pissed off. Or maybe that was the strobe light.

I must have looked so glum, as Duke used to say, with

my chin on my hands and my elbows on my thighs, right next to Gina Glum. I can't believe I turned down Sydney Holland. I bet she and Miranda laughed their faces off at what a gigantic mistake I made.

Me and Gina sat there for 23 minutes total. The whole time, Hunk pressed against Phoebe from *Friends* like they were Siamese twins. And Sydney wouldn't even look back in my direction.

Then Heather rushed over to us, grabbed Gina by the arm and yelled "Bathroom!" and ran off with her. I had no idea what was happening until Nate came over with this mondo grin on his face like he'd just scored. He goes, "Did you see it? Did you see it?" practically shouting. I'm like, "See what?"

Nate filled me in. They were dancing to "La Bamba." Everyone was waving their hands in the air and jumping around. Heather got really into it, and the whole top part of her dress slid to her waist. Before she could pull her dress back up and run off, Nate got to see both boobs—completely everything, close up.

He said they looked like tennis balls. Not green and fuzzy, but just as bouncy and round and perfect. Why wasn't I looking!

Nate and I were giving each other high fives when someone pounded on my shoulder. I turned around and faced Hunk. He goes, "Hey, Storky, are you Gina's date?"

I thought, This is how I die. A 220-pound lineman beats the life out of me, and I haven't even kissed a girl yet or learned to drive. In my head I said, Yeah, I'm Gina's date, you got a problem with that, Jockula? Instead I nodded and looked at my shoes.

He goes, "Poser." Then he walked away. All I could think was, Thank God he didn't beat me up. I'm such a wimp. Still haven't figured out what a poser is. It can't be good.

When the girls came back, Nate and Heather headed off to take pictures. He held her hand. Her other hand was like glued to the top of her dress.

Gina went back to staring at Hunk and Phoebe. They practically had dry sex to the theme song from *Titanic*. I hate that song anyway.

I kept looking for Sydney, but couldn't find her anywhere. With my luck, she was probably in a dark corner making out with some guy. Just as I was picturing that, Hunk slid Phoebe right in front of Gina, grabbed the back of Phoebe's head, and kissed her. A long one. Likely involving tongue.

That's when Gina goes, "I can't do this anymore." She started begging me to go home. So I said, "Fine, we'll ask Nate to call his mom next time we see him." What am I supposed to say—No, you have to suffer here with me all night? Then I guess Gina got so desperate she went out searching for him. I followed her like a stupid puppy.

We found Nate and Heather on the folding chairs on the far side of the auditorium, totally lip-locked. I could tell he was pissed when Gina asked him to call his mom.

So that's pretty much how that crappy night ended. Oh yeah, one more crappy thing. The Mike Wallace thing. The whole way home, Nate's mom—who's usually the weak, silent type—fired off a ton of questions. How was the restaurant? How was the dance? Were your friends there? Did you get your pictures taken? Why did you leave so early? I wanted to shove a couple cigarettes in her mouth and tell her to mind her own business.

So that's it. That's it for my night. That's it for the Snowball. That's it for school dances. That's it for me and Gina. That's it for me and any girl. That's it for me.

And I still have 13 more days before I get the TV back.

Monday, December 20

It's *Winter Break, Unplugged.* 11 more days of TV deprivation. Read *Ethan Frome* today. Compared to that guy, or anyone in that book, my life's a total picnic.

Thursday, December 23

Met Nate at the mall. He's going to a party with Heather on New Year's Eve, so he bought a 5-pack of condoms at Rite Aid. They sure make a lot of different kinds—ribbed, lubricated, extra strength, Valupaks. He just got the regular Trojans, because that's the only one we've heard of.

The lady at the register looked about 110 years old. She could practically be Grandma's grandma. Even Nate was blushing and fumbling with his money in front of her. As she was ringing him up, she goes, "Good for you, sonny.

Take it from me. You don't want herpes." We were so freaked, we didn't even wait for Nate's change.

Nate's cousin works at Pretzel Time, so we got free pretzels and Cokes. Then we went over to Hickory Farms and tasted like 5 different cheeses plus a salami. For dessert, we each took a couple handfuls of cookie samples from Mrs. Fields. I didn't spend a dime all day.

Tonight Amanda's date was more than 15 minutes late, so she ditched him and drove over to Bulimic Michele's house. On her way out, Amanda goes, "Just let my date know tardies are inexcusable." Harsh!

When the guy finally showed up, Vermin made him sit on the flowery couch while he grilled him about his intentions with Amanda and his future career goals and stuff. After the grilling, Verm told the poor jerk that Amanda wasn't there. As soon as he left, me and Verm started busting up. Mom made clicking noises and shook her head.

Friday, December 24

Begged for the TV back 8 days early, since it's winter break and I'm dying of boredom. I'm halfway through *War and Peace.* 703 more pages to go. Mom's being a hard-ass. Says if I finish it *and Anna Karenina,* she might reconsider. Says if I'm so bored, I should go to Golden Village. No way.

Saturday, December 25

Christmas is hard when you're a Jew. Nothing's open. Everyone else is eating fruitcake and stringing popcorn or whatever with their families. Being Jewish on Christmas doesn't stop Amanda from being all social. Bulimic Michele had her over. I wonder if she threw up her Christmas dinner. Spewed cranberry sauce. Gross.

I was so bored today, I agreed to catch a movie with Mom and Verm. That's about the one good thing you can do on Christmas—go to the movie theater and see everyone from temple. Either that or watch all the dads on the block help their kids ride their new bikes and scooters and stuff.

Verm vetoed Mom's movie choice. He won't see anything with Meryl Streep, especially if she's doing an accent. Me and Verm picked this war film. I didn't understand it, but the battle stuff was cool. I fell asleep near the end. Woke up to Mom and Verm holding hands. Ugh.

We went to Denny's afterward. It was the only thing open. All these families sat in the booths, dressed up in fancy red-and-green outfits, eating sliced turkey and mashed potatoes and gravy. It just seems so depressing. Your big holiday dinner spent at Denny's.

I wonder what Duke's doing for Christmas.

Sunday, December 26

I'm so sick of Dad being late. It's like I'm the lowest priority in his life. After I waited 38 minutes for him, I pulled an Amanda. I ditched the house and biked over to Nate's. I told him Dad canceled. I didn't feel like going all into it.

We watched *SportsCenter* and the *Real World* marathon.

We're going to drive to L.A. and try out for *Real World* when we're 18. They should take me. They need a dweeb on the show. I'm sick of those cool guys they always have, sitting in their Jacuzzis and whining about how hard it is to handle all their girlfriends.

I hope Dad calls the house all night long, and Mom and Amanda don't get home until late, and Dad wonders if he'll ever see me again. Knowing Dad, he probably just shrugged or something and went to dinner without me.

If I ever get married and have kids, I'll be a great dad. I'll never be late for anything. I'll be one of those guys who coaches Little League and goes to the park with his family every weekend. I won't go out of town on business trips all the time, especially so that my kid, thinking back, wonders if they really were business trips after all.

Monday, December 27

This vacation bites. I almost miss school. I was so bored today, I played Scrabble alone. Even challenged myself on the word *zim*. Gina might have been up for a game, but no way am I calling her. I'm still too pissed off. I wonder how her Christmas was.

Glad I decided to ditch Dad yesterday. Leaving the house before he got there wasn't exactly standing up to him though. At least I did something. At least I took The Road Not Taken. Maybe he'll respect me now. Maybe he'll say how mature I am and offer to buy me a car.

Yeah, right. I'm just a wuss who snuck out of the house before he showed up. Like I ran out on Duke before he could tell me anything about Dad.

Tuesday, December 28

Decided to take another Road Not Taken. Decided to apologize to Duke. Decided even if Duke tells me off for being a jerk, I'm man enough to go see him. Tagged along with Mom.

The old people were so excited to see us, it was sad. Mom did the ladies' nails and showed off the pictures of me in my Snowball suit and Amanda in her slinky dress. Some of the old men really got a kick out of the Amanda pictures.

Duke ignored us. Kept his eyes on the newspaper. Must be weird to read about the world from a nursing home.

He didn't look up until I said, "I'm sorry, Duke." He folded the newspaper and set it on his lap. Then he bobbed his head at me and goes, "That's all right, I was once a teenager myself."

I tried to calculate how many years ago that was—70, 75? I thought, Maybe it's okay my life is so messed up now. If I'm lucky, I have another 75 years or so to overcome it.

We played Scrabble for 3 straight hours. Long after Mom left. She had to come back and get me later. He beat me every game.

That's okay. It wasn't just Scrabble tips. Never was, I guess. He asked how the dance went, and I unloaded on him. How I like Gina so much, but she's rebounding. He mostly just listened.

Except about half a game after I told him all that, he said, "Can I tell you something about your so-called friend Gina, without you running off again?" I go, "So-called?" He crossed his flabby arms and frowned at me until I said, "I won't run off again, just tell me." So he said, "She's not worth it." He told me how inconsiderate she was for sulking all night and making the rest of us leave early. I said, "She was miserable, remember? Remember I told you she cried in the bathroom?" He goes, still frowning, "I don't like her."

Then he said she must have me totally distracted if I'd use my *z* for a little word like *zoo* and leave it open for him. He put *zirconia* over a triple word score for 107 points.

If he could meet Gina and see her bright dark eyes and her little wrists and shoulders, he'd realize how sweet she really is. Not that she'd ever set foot in Golden Village.

Wednesday, December 29

It sucks when you like someone more than they like you. Gina called to make sure I had no hard feelings about the Snowball. To make sure I understood. That's what she said. She wasn't trying to ruin my night, she said.

Even though I've been mad at her all week, I told her I understood. I asked her if she was feeling better. Even while I pictured Duke shaking his head in disgust, I asked about her Christmas.

To make it even worse, I invited her over to play Scrabble and she turned me down. Now I'm not only mad at Gina, I'm mad at myself too. What a loser. Though I bet I would have beaten her.

Thursday, December 30

Dr. Vermin's over all the time now. Ever since Mom started winter break from law school, she just hangs with Verm every day. He had dinner here again tonight.

Just when I'm thinking he's not such a bad dude, I hear them arguing in Mom's bedroom. He complained how he never gets to sleep over and how he's not driving home on New Year's Eve with all the drunks on the road, and then Mom brought me into it. The whole fight turned out to be because of me. She doesn't want to set a bad example. She goes, "Even if Amanda could handle it, Mike's always been so sensitive." I hate that. She says I still have issues from the Divorce. I hate that too. Pulling out all the psychological crap and fighting about me behind my back.

It's not psychological. I just don't want him sleeping over. I don't want him seeing me in my bathrobe. I don't want to have to eat breakfast with him. I don't want to share the Sports section with him. I don't want any more people in this house using up the hot water before I can take my shower. I don't want him having sex with Mom in the bed Dad used to sleep in.

Saturday, January 1

I love TV! I zoned in front of it today for like 12 straight hours. Rose Bowl! Sugar Bowl! Fiesta Bowl! And tomorrow the national championship game! Life is good!

Even last night worked out okay. Weird, but okay. It was just me and Mom at first, both of us pretty bummed. Nate was out with Heather Kvaas and those condoms. Amanda went to another popular-seniors-only party. Mom sat on the couch, biting her nails and leafing through this stack of *Good Housekeeping* magazines Grandma gave her. Verm wouldn't come over because he didn't want to drive home on New Year's Eve.

I got Mom to go bowling with me. I figured if anyone at school saw me out with her on New Year's Eve, they'd be just as embarrassed because they'd be at the bowling alley too. We picked up Aunt Marsha on the way. We were like this lonely losers gang. I felt so crappy I only bowled a 133 the first game.

I was trolling the place for other pathetic teenagers when about 8 lanes down I saw Verm. He looked even more pitiful than us, being all by himself.

At first I thought it was a setup, like when Dad used to pretend to accidentally bump into his girlfriends when he was out with me. But then Mom got all nervous when I pointed him out, and she didn't want to go over there.

Aunt Marsha said it was karma. I didn't say anything. Mom kept looking at Vermin every 5 seconds. It was like Gina and Hunk at the Snowball all over again. Ugh.

Finally, Aunt Marsha did this loud whistle, with her fingers in her mouth and everything, and yelled, "Howard!" Mom said, "Marsha" and shook her head, but actually she seemed pretty glad.

When he saw us, he like sprinted to our lane. He gave Mom this big hug, and they went, "I'm sorry," "No, I'm sorry," "No, I'm sorry," like a *7th Heaven* episode, with Aunt Marsha smiling and me just wanting to ralph.

Another night spent with the Vermster. After we bowled a second game, Dr. Vermin got up to leave, and he and Mom fell all over each other going, "Happy New Year," and "I'll call," and "I'm sorry" again.

Something made me tell Mom, "Just let him sleep over, I can handle it." I guess it's because I didn't like seeing Mom all bummed last night. Or possibly I'm getting mature. Or maybe I wanted a real *7th Heaven* ending where everyone works everything out and there's a gazillion people living in one house without anyone ever fighting over the bathroom or who left out the dirty dishes.

Mom tried to have this big heart-to-heart with me about whether it was really okay, blah blah blah. But I could tell she was tired, and I'm not a big talker anyway. So me and Aunt Marsha convinced her to just go home with Dr. Vermin while we stayed to bowl the third game.

Aunt Marsha's pretty okay. We got some chili cheese fries in the coffee shop afterward, and I told her the whole pathetic story of the Snowball, and how I wimped out Tuesday with Gina on the phone.

Somehow I got to talking about Dad. I don't know, it felt good to tell someone. And since she calls him The Pig sometimes, I figured she'd understand. She didn't really. She said even though he's a pig, he's still my dad.

Then she told me a long story about this guy who sits at the dock watching all the boats go by and never gets on one because he's afraid of the water, and then a tidal wave knocks him off the dock and drowns him. That story somehow means I'm supposed to call Dad and Gina and tell them they should be nicer to me.

Aunt Marsha patted my hand and said if I ever needed to talk, I could come over to her place and she'd make that tofu prune casserole I liked so much. It got way too cheesy, so I go, "Since you want me to be honest, I hate tofu." She laughed and said we could just order out for pizza next time.

I ended up sleeping until 11:09 this morning. By the time I went downstairs for breakfast, Dr. Vermin was just walking out the door. So him sleeping over was no big deal after all.

But I hope he only does it on New Year's and maybe Mom's birthday. This better not get out of control. I don't want them living together or anything.

Sunday, January 2

Big phone call day. I called Dad, Nate, and Gina. Luckily Dad wasn't there or he was screening, so I left him a message.

Been calling Nate for the last 2 days to find out if he got lucky on New Year's Eve. I wonder why he's not calling back.

I wrote down what to say to Gina, but on the phone it didn't come out that well. Said I was bummed about the Snowball, how she blew me off. Because it was my night too, not just hers. Gina apologized. But she didn't seem sorry. It was more like she said it to shut me up.

I could have told her about Sydney Holland, that I wish I hadn't turned her down, that while Gina was sighing over Hunk and Phoebe from *Friends,* I was watching Sydney all happy on the dance floor, with her long legs and sparkly eyes.

But I couldn't even say Sydney's name. Maybe because it's mean to tell one girl that you think another girl's hot— even though Gina's always gushing over Hunk in front of me. Or maybe I knew Gina would bring up Sydney's braces, or her frizzy hair, or her barrettes. Maybe because Sydney and Gina are in different leagues. And I mean that as a compliment to Sydney.

Monday, January 3

When Dad called me back today, I was all set to ask him to be more on time. I'd written the whole thing down, just like Aunt Marsha said to do. But he just bawled me out.

He kept saying he was only a half hour late last week, which is just plain bull, because I timed it on my Seiko watch that he gave me for middle school graduation, and it was at

least 38 minutes. Anyway, why should he be even a half hour late? Maybe I have better things to do than sit home and look out the window every 2 minutes for his Lexus.

He goes how he works so hard to pay child support so Mom doesn't have to work, and I remembered this fight they had before the Divorce when Mom was studying for the LSAT. Dad said she was too old for law school and she'd never last there and she should clean the house instead of wasting all her time on one goddamn test.

I'm so sick of it all. Everything. I gave him the Gina treatment, the I'm-sorry-just-to-get-this-person-off-my-back apology.

I bet he'll be late next time. Just to make a point. Maybe I won't show up again. Or maybe I'll grow a backbone and tell him off. Sure. Right after I tell off Gina.

Tuesday, January 4

Nate finally called back. He won't tell me whether he got laid or not. I guess some guys wouldn't tell if they did, just out of respect for the girl. I'd probably be like that, if I ever did have sex. But I can't see Nate being all respectful.

I bet he didn't get any. Heather and Gina could have like a best friends pact to keep their virginities. Or maybe there was no place to do it at the party. Maybe the parents stayed home or all the bedrooms were filled with other people having sex. Or maybe Heather wanted her first time with Nate to be in a really romantic place like a motel room.

Wednesday, January 5

I might be overdoing the TV a little. Haven't been out of the house in 5 days.

Thursday, January 6

I have to admit 2 things. One, I'm getting a little sick of TV. Two, in a weird way I'm looking forward to school starting Monday.

What if Nate and Heather are a total couple by now, and I sit with them and Gina at the popular table this semester, and people stop calling me Storky? Highly doubtful. At least school will force me out of the house though.

Law school starts next week too. I'm real psyched for that. Mom's been in my face, nagging me every day to get off my butt. The omniscient voice, as Ms. Dore says in Honors English.

Plus the Vermster is here all the time now. He even slept over last night. It wasn't totally bad. He bought a dozen Krispy Kremes this morning. I ate 4. Verm only had 2. Amanda didn't leave her room.

Friday, January 7

Saw Duke today. He beat me by more than 70 points both games. I don't know if it's the furniture or the people or what, but the air in Golden Village smells about 50 years old, like you don't want to take a deep breath.

While I was there, this guy who looked a little older than

Dad visited this crinkly old lady. He kept saying, "It's me, Mama, your son Donny." The old lady just stared ahead like she was watching a movie. She patted the guy's hand, but you could tell she had no clue. It was the most pathetic thing I've seen in a long time.

Duke said that it isn't so bad being in a wheelchair and stuff, but that if he ever loses his mind, I should shoot him. He says they don't convict people for mercy killing. He used to be a D.A., so he knows. For a guy who's a gazillion years old, he's pretty cool.

I want to die instantly of a brain seizure when I'm 52.

Sunday, January 9

Got to see real-live, almost-naked ladies tonight. Seeing Dad though was as wacked as usual. At least he only came 18 minutes late.

He took me to a little theater downtown. It didn't even have heating, so everyone had to watch this boring play with their arms crossed over their chests and shivering. It was supposed to be in the future. The stage was full of trash, and the actors wore gas masks and made long speeches about how they just wanted a ticket to live on the moon. It was so lame.

Afterward we had to go backstage and meet Dad's new bimbo delight or whatever she is. She was the first one to get a ticket to the moon. The moon trip turned out to be a big lie, and all the ticket holders got killed instead. She told Dad it was supposed to be like the 80s in America, and Dad nodded like his head was falling off his neck and used the word *edgy* about 100 times.

I hope he was only trying to make her feel good. He didn't really like the play, did he? He probably just wanted to make the moves on her. She's pretty sexy. She has long red hair and big boobs for a skinny lady. Dad told her his Boomer Esiason story and she not only knew who he was, she goes, "That's so fabulous."

They pretty much ignored me. Which was excellent, actually. Considering the dinky theater didn't have any dressing rooms. The actors and actresses hung around backstage, some of them still changing. I saw 2 guys in their boxers, plus 3 girls in their bras and underwear. They didn't seem embarrassed at all. I just kept trying to keep Rex under control. The whole time I was there, the tall Asian actress sat on the wood floor, chain-smoking in her bra and panties, talking to some dressed dude. She must have been cold. I knew if I looked closer to see if her nipples were hard, Rex would go half mast for sure. I was already listing European capitals just to contain him. I want to be an actor when I grow up.

Monday, January 10

As soon as my first class started today, with Mr. Whitehead droning on and on about the amazing atom and the mighty molecule while the jarhead in front of me stuck his gum in Jordan Newman's hair, I realized what an idiot I was for wanting school to start up again.

Lunch sucked the most of the whole day. Even Aunt

Marsha's yam surprise tastes better than the crapeteria's sloppy joes. Nate acted all sad and quiet about whatever went on with Heather. Gina walked toward me at the beginning of lunch period like she was going to sit with me. Just as I started going into shock, these 2 JV cheerleaders at the A-list table yelled, "Gina! What are you doing with Storky Pomerantz? We saved you a place here!" Gina couldn't get to them fast enough.

After lunch sucked too. When Sydney came into Spanish class and saw me sitting in the back left corner, she rushed past me to the front right corner.

Plus, Ms. Padilla announced that we have to do team projects on Spanish culture. Ugh. What does culture have to do with speaking Spanish? If they got rid of all the lame homework that doesn't help anyone learn, and stopped teaching totally useless subjects like ancient history and geometry, we could finish high school in one year.

And I hate team projects. They always mean one person doing all the work and the other person just taking the good grade. Of course, I'm the one who does all the work. The combination of being smart, a grade hound, and a wuss automatically makes me the worker half of the team.

How could I have ever forgotten how much school sucks?

Thursday, January 13

48 more school days until spring break. If it weren't for Martin Luther King Day and the dead presidents' days, I don't think I could take the wait.

Nate's been quiet all week. He's no fun anymore. He won't say what's going on. Amanda said she heard all about Nate, that Gina and Heather are big gossips, and I shouldn't waste my time on them. But she wouldn't tell me anything else. Some sister. Does the whole school know except me?

WHAT COULD HAVE HAPPENED TO NATE AND HEATHER

1. Parents walked in on them.
2. Nate got real drunk and ralphed on Heather.
3. Vice versa.
4. Nate decided he wants to be a virgin after all.
5. He got his johnson stuck in his zipper, like in *There's Something About Mary.*
6. Heather's really a guy, like in *Mrs. Doubtfire.*
7. Nate's really a girl, like in *Boys Don't Cry.*

Friday, January 14

Ms. Padilla assigned the teams for our stupid Spanish culture projects today. She said it was to save time, but I think she did it out of spite. As she read the names, you could see the look of terror on people. Like she paired Jenny Rennert, homecoming princess, with Amy Kantnor, who has oily hair and zits. And Mark Rudolph, JV quarterback, with Stuart O'Donnell, skinny computer geek. Then she called out Sydney Holland's name, and I knew, I just knew she'd put her with me. And she did. Why? Why is my life made up of stuff like this?

112

Just to really torture us, Padilla said we're meeting with our partners on Tuesday, so we can have the whole long weekend to sweat it out. We're supposed to do an oral report on Spanish food, clothes, art, plays, or movies. Any guy teacher would let us do sports. I'd give a report on *futbol* anytime. Maybe a bio of Pele. Now that would be cool.

I bet Sydney makes me go to some girly thing, like a Spanish play or an art museum. I'd do it too, as long as she kept quiet about the Rex Incident and the Snowball. Except no way am I dressing up like a tango dancer.

Saturday, January 15

I think Berm told me more personal stuff today than Dad's said all year. Is that pathetic or what? Berm's practically a member of the family now. He sleeps here like every weekend.

Mom and Amanda had a big fight over it. It started this morning when Amanda walked in on him on the can. I wonder if he was sitting or standing at the time? Sitting would probably be better. She might not have seen much if he was taking a dump. Maybe he has a really big johnson. Maybe that's why Mom likes him.

Amanda screamed how she has no privacy with Dr. Berman around, and no one ever asked her if he could move in, and it's bad enough with me laying on the couch all the time with the TV blaring. How she can't even walk into a bathroom in private.

Then Mom shouted that she had to have a life too, besides cleaning up after Amanda like a maid and taking her phone messages like a secretary while Amanda's out on dates every night.

They just had to drag me into it. Amanda said Mom wanted her to be a social feeb like me, and Mom goes maybe if she was less social she'd have grades like mine, and Amanda said Mom always stuck up for me and that's why I'm such a wimp.

I left the house. I slammed the door hard, either to show them I wasn't a wimp or just because I was mad, I don't know which.

Berman followed right after and put his arm around me like he's my dad or something. I squirmed out of the way. I walked for about a block, with Berman trailing, before I let him catch up.

He goes, "You think there's any way I could get Amanda on my good side?" I thought of 2 answers. First, Amanda's not on anyone's good side. Second, Stop seeing Mom, and Amanda will be fine. But I didn't say anything. I didn't feel like being a smartass. I just practiced soccer kicks with rocks as I walked.

Then he said, "I'm in love with your mother." I guess I knew that already. I guess I should have felt pissed, instead of just glad for her.

He went on. "And I think you and Amanda are terrific." I didn't feel at all terrific. Not after just hearing Amanda cut me down. I kicked a rock that was more like a boulder, stubbing my toe. I tried not to show I was hurt. As I limped up the street, I said, "I'm a social feeb, according to my terrific sister." Then Berm goes, "You know, even though your sister may have more friends, you seem to have a close friend in Nate. Sometimes that's better."

Complete bull. It's always better to be popular. Plus, the way things have been going with Nate, I wouldn't call him such a close friend right now.

Then Berm goes, "I'm not out to take your dad's place." And I said, "Dad's not exactly Mike Brady."

Berm didn't say anything. He tried to kick a rock, but he tripped over himself. I couldn't help it, I laughed. And he joined in. It was more like a laugh of relief, like when you get out a good belch after a big dinner.

He put his arm around me again, and I let it stay for about 90 seconds before moving away. It felt pretty good, in a fake way. As long as I didn't think he was just some dude screwing my mom, it felt okay.

He goes, "He might not be Mike Brady, but he's still your father." Aunt Marsha said the same thing about Dad, but Amanda says he's just the sperm donor. I guess Dad's more than just a sperm donor, but less of a dad than Mike Brady. Somewhere in the middle.

As for Berman, he's less important than Dad but nicer. Where that leaves him I'm clueless. But I don't need to figure it out right now. I have enough on my mind with the Sydney Holland Spanish project coming up, and Mom and Amanda screaming in the kitchen.

Though when Berm and I got back to the house, Mom and Amanda were eating breakfast together. Well, actually Amanda just ate grapefruit because she's on another diet, and Mom sat at the table scraping black stuff from the Eggo she'd burned.

Tuesday, January 18

Met with Sydney Holland today in Spanish class. It wasn't as bad as I thought. She didn't mention the Rex Incident. Or the Snowball. Phew!

In fact, she was kind of nice. Actually, very nice. She asked me what project I wanted to do. I suggested the Pele bio, and she said that sounded okay but that we better ask the teacher.

Sydney might be as into grades as me. Maybe I won't have to do all the work this time. And she might be the one girl in high school who's impressed by a smart guy. Maybe her dream date is Captain Sensitive.

Ms. Padilla immediately vetoed my Pele idea. Of course.

Then Sydney came up with this awful plan. She said she read this enchanting novel, *Like Water for Chocolate*, about these sisters and their mother. The enchanting book had enchanting recipes in it and was made into an enchanting movie. She wanted to rent the movie and cook one of the dishes.

Yuck. Enchanting movie about sisters and mom = chick flick. And cooking on top of that. Then to have to stand up in class and talk about seeing a girl movie and cooking. Total humiliation.

But I was worried about saying no and making Sydney mad. She could tell people about the Rex Incident. I decided to risk it and suggested Plan B, which was to eat tacos and talk about it. I thought we could go to Taco Bell, Jack in the Box, and some other fast-food place, doing like a taco taste test and making it all scientific.

When I started telling Sydney my plan about eating out, she got all psyched before I could mention the fast-food part of it. She wants to go to this Mexican restaurant in Old Town that's supposed to be real authentic. Eduardo's. She heard Mercedes Bonnafeux all excited about it on the radio when her dad was driving her to a swim meet. Sydney's probably the only other person my age who knows about Mercedes Bonnafeux.

I was just relieved not to see that chick flick and cook, and not to explain the Rex Incident. So I nodded my head up and down like a drill while she talked, even when she said it was A Bit Pricey.

What does A Bit Pricey mean? Probably a lot more than the cost of 3 fast-food tacos. I have that money Dad gave me for the suit. But I was saving it for computer games.

Sydney doesn't expect me to pay for both of us, does she? Is this like a date? Or payback for keeping quiet about the Rex Incident? Maybe Sydney thinks it's a date. She seemed all excited. She said she'd drive. Is it a date if the girl drives and you're doing it for Spanish class? No. That's insane.

I need to stop thinking of everything like a date. The Snowball, for instance. That was just me helping out a friend. Former friend, anyway.

Thursday, January 20

It's totally over with Gina. Not that anything ever was, but my part of it is over. She called. For a favor. The only reason she ever calls. Could I tell her about *Of Mice and Men* so she could write a halfway-decent essay? She never read it, and Blockbuster didn't carry the DVD. She goes, "Which one is George and which is Lenny, and what's up with the rabbit?"

I almost cried during that book it was so good. Okay, I did cry. I told her, "If you come over today, I'll lend you a copy and you can at least skim it." Then she goes, "I can't. I promised Hunk I'd go to the beach with him."

I said, "It's like 50 degrees out, what are you going to the beach for?" For a smart guy I'm so dumb. When she didn't answer, when chirpy little Gina went silent, I realized what she and the Incredible Hunk were doing at the beach. Finally, she goes, "So is George the smart redneck or the dumb one?"

I couldn't help it. I said, "You're doing it with him, aren't you?" Then she goes, "It's none of your business." She said, "Lots of people our age have sex, you know. Nate and Heather were going to on New Year's Eve, except your friend Nate couldn't even get it up." She let out a laugh and said, "I wonder if he's old enough for Viagra." She got all excited to talk about him, but it made me feel grungy hearing it.

I never guessed it before, that Nate couldn't perform that night. I can see how he would feel embarrassed. Maybe he was too nervous, or drunk. Maybe it's like the poetry report—Nate doesn't do well under pressure. I don't know. It's not something Heather should have told people about, I know that.

And not something Gina should have repeated. I might not be popular, but I know about being a friend. I know Nate felt bad about what happened, but Gina gushed over it like an actress plugging her newest movie. Like she used the Nate/Heather story so I wouldn't think about her putting out just to stay with a dumb jock.

And she wouldn't let up. "Have you heard Nate's new nickname?" she asked, and I couldn't help cringing just thinking about people calling me Storky. She waited for me to ask what it was, but I didn't. She told me anyway. "It's Gimp. Get it? Because he's like sexually crippled."

I could get more creative than that, I thought. In 3 minutes. But I wouldn't. Because I felt sorry for Nate.

And Gina's the one who should have felt bad. For opening up her mouth about Nate. And hooking up with big Hunk, with his monster hands and clunky head.

I couldn't wait to get her off the phone. "So, about *Of Mice and Men,*" I said. "Yeah, can you give me like a 3-minute summary?" she asked. I wasn't about to make it any easier for Gina to go to the beach with Hunk. Or cheat in English class. Or skip a Steinbeck novel. Anyway, how could I explain that George shot Lenny as a mark of their friendship? I don't think Gina knows the first thing about friendship. "I didn't read it," I lied. "Can't help you this time."

Gina was like, "Really? Michael A. Pomerantz actually didn't do an assignment?" She sounded impressed. And I thought how screwed up she was to be impressed with that. "Really, I didn't," I lied again.

Then I realized something else about her. "You don't keep a journal anymore, do you?" I said. And she's like, "No. That was my stupid sensitive phase. I'm too busy now. With Hunk and friends and stuff." I go, "I thought so." Then I added, "Have fun tonight" before hanging up the phone.

Now I'm sitting here in front of the computer in my Chargers pajamas with the brown football-shaped slippers Aunt Marsha gave me for Hanukkah, and I'm feeling better. Relieved almost. Feeling like I smartened up.

I guess I wasted all those years thinking I loved her. And I blew all that money on her for the necklace, and the cab fare after her fight with Hunk, and the Snowball.

And actually Gina's nothing. Definitely pretty. And smart. And popular. But nothing really. Not even as good as bitchy Amanda, who at least stands up for herself with boyfriends and doesn't gossip. Or Nate, who might be sort of a loser popularity-wise, but is a loyal friend.

Definitely not as good as Sydney. She never told about the Rex Incident. Never once reminded me of it afterward. Only gave a laugh that day and said, "Oh my God, Mike." She never told, and I bet she'd never have sex with a dumb idiot just so he wouldn't break up with her. She might not be as pretty as Gina, but she's got brains. And she does have really nice green eyes, and that cute dimple on her right cheek. Or is it her left? I'll check tomorrow.

Saturday, January 22

Slept over at Nate's last night. His mom was at her newest boyfriend's house. Some dude she met in a bar.

I'm glad I told him I know what happened. Now we're total buds again. 100% agreement that Heather and Gina are horrible for telling everyone. I go, "Maybe you would have scored if Heather didn't look like such a boy." Which is a lie. Heather's a total babe. But I think Nate might have bought it.

We got so trashed. Nate swiped his mom's tequila from the kitchen cupboard. We didn't have any limes or soda or anything, so we mixed it with Kool-Aid. Wasn't bad after about the first glass.

Nate says his mom's a vodka drinker, so it'll be a while before she notices. The important thing is my mom didn't find out. Plus, after having a bulldozer in my head all morning, my hangover's finally gone.

For someone so cool, it's weird he couldn't keep it up New Year's Eve. It's like him bombing the poetry report last semester. Nate says he can't come through in a clinch. Which led to me joking that not coming was the least of his problems, and somehow us going to the backyard for a pissing contest. I won for accuracy. Nate won for distance. I hope his mom's roses don't die.

To cheer him up and also because I was drunk, I told him all about the Rex Incident. Actually, unloading on him made me feel better too. I don't know if it was the tequila or what, but we now have new nicknames. Nate's is L.D. and mine is S.D. Limpdick and Stickdick. It was way funnier last night.

We're going to lift weights together. I hate that kind of stuff, basically anything getting me off my butt. But it'll be worth it to get big muscles.

We'll get so pumped, Heather and Gina will eat their hearts out. Their cold little hearts. And after we get all strong, Nate's going to track down his dad and force him to pay the child support he owes, and I'll show my dad he can't push me around.

Sunday, January 23

Couldn't even watch TV in peace today. Mom and her new law school friend Chad were practicing for moot court, pacing around the living room all serious and intense.

The guy looks like a male model. And a lot younger than Berm, like 25, with a Swatch watch and dyed blond tips. I can't see spending any time or money on hair dye, but maybe that's just me.

They wanted me to hear their speeches. I go, "Mom, why don't you call your *boyfriend* and have *him* listen." She said, "Don't worry about Chad, hon." Then they gave each other these big meaningful stares into each other's eyes and superior smiles like they had something to hide. Mom's like,

"Chad and I are just friends." And they both laughed, and Mom said, "I'm glad you're feeling so protective about Howard, but Howard and I are doing just fine." I go, "No, that's not it." But I sort of suspected maybe it was.

So I had to hear Mom and Chad argue about whether someone can turn off your ventilator when you're a vegetable. Seems obvious to me. If I was a turnip, I wouldn't want to lie around drooling and wearing a diaper while everyone sat around my hospital bed grossing out. It's like what Duke said: Once your brain goes, you should be shot dead.

When I couldn't take being around Mom and Chad one more minute, I biked to Golden Village. Duke sat in the Community Room surrounded by a harem of old ladies laughing all over themselves like he was the Last Comic Standing. Or sitting. While the blue-haired lady read his palm, he made some lame sex joke about having big hands and a big johnny. All I could think of were the Hunk's big hands and little Gina. Duke was so right about her.

He didn't want to play Scrabble. He was psyched that it was so sunny and asked me to push his chair around outside. I'd just been outside. I had to bike all the way over to see him. Plus I'm not one of those outdoorsy types. Give me a choice between staying in a heated house with a TV or going on a nature walk, you know where I'll be. But I couldn't turn down an old man in a wheelchair.

I told him about Gina, and he didn't even say I told you so. He goes, "Don't worry. You're the type of guy who gets more attractive with age." I'm like, "What, you think getting all bald and wrinkled will be an improvement?" He points to my head, and goes, "As girls mature, they realize the brain is the sexiest part of the male body."

Hmm. It certainly isn't the sexiest part of the female body. Boobs, legs, eyes, hair, and like 10 other body parts are way hotter than a brain. But I think I know what Duke was saying. He means after girls get burned by a few lardheads, they start concentrating on the squids. Like me.

Plus, Duke said skinny guys such as myself supposedly fill out a little, while the bigger dudes just get fat. I wonder when this happens. At least not until after college, I bet. Well, what's another 7½ more years of misery.

Duke says when you get old like him, the ladies really come after you—because most of the other guys your age are dead. And if you have any money, like he does, they practically worship you. I guess growing all old does have its good points. Except I don't know if getting worshiped by women is so great if they have blue hair, or no teeth, or keep forgetting who you are.

If I had a cool car, it would help with girls. Duke doesn't really relate. He says in his day hardly anyone owned cars.

I wonder what kind of car Chad drives. Probably nothing as cool as Berm's Jeep.

Wednesday, January 26

Went to the moot court competition. Mom and Chad won! They're the best pretend lawyers in the whole school. They stood on stage arguing in front of 3 real judges and hundreds of people in the audience. The other team was these 2 macho blowhards, and Mom and Chad kicked their butts. Mom got all smart and loud. I couldn't believe it. Her genes probably helped me ace the poetry report last semester.

Berm gave her a standing ovation. Aunt Marsha did one of her wolf whistles. I clapped so much my hands got red. Even Amanda quit looking at her watch and cheered for Mom.

Afterward we got pie at Applebee's. Not Amanda, because she's on a diet. Except she had so many bites of everyone else's pie that if you added it up, she probably ate at least a slice and a half. I don't know why girls are always going on and off their stupid diets.

Oh, yeah. Chad came too. With his domestic partner, as he called him. Troy, a hairdresser. Okay, I'm dumb. So that's why Mom laughed at me for getting jealous. Why was I jealous anyway? Dr. Berm must be growing on me. Like mold.

At Applebee's, Aunt Marsha goes, "Geraldine, you've always been a wonderful big sister. And now here you are, managing law school, 2 teenagers, and a boyfriend, all with such grace and style."

I doubt the words *Geraldine, grace,* and *style* have ever been used in the same sentence before. I mean, it's pretty obvious Mom gave me my extensive collection of dweeb genes. But tonight she did seem graceful and stylish. Awesome, actually.

I got carried away. When we came home, I dug up that old *G* necklace I bought for Gina, still wrapped up, even, and gave it to Mom. Really, what else could I do with it? How many girls' names start with G besides Gina and Geraldine?

Besides, Mom deserved it. I told her I was proud of her. She got all teary and said hearing me say that was even better than hearing the judges announce her name tonight. Screwy!

Then she said she was proud of me for visiting Duke and doing so well in school. And not drinking anymore. I grabbed the remote and turned on the TV real loud.

Sunday, January 30

WORST THINGS ABOUT NIGHT WITH DAD

1. He came 26 minutes late.
2. He wore this Spider-man baseball cap backward.
3. He talked on his cell phone the whole way to the restaurant.
4. It was an Indian restaurant.
5. That actress from the sucky play met us there.
6. He didn't seem to care that Mom won the moot court contest.
7. He said he won't buy me a car.

Friday, February 4

One of the best nights I've had in a long time. Went out with Sydney. Not like on a date. We went to Eduardo's for our report. Whoever knew working on a Spanish culture team project could be so fantastic? It was perfect.

Well, forking over $25 for my part of the dinner wasn't perfect, especially since the food didn't taste any better than what you could get for 5 bucks at Taco Bell. Actually, my part of the bill was only $23.77, but I didn't want to look cheap. Aside from the money factor, it was *totalmente perfecto*.

She came to the house exactly on time. And looking really pretty. She wore this tight yellow sweater. Very tight. She has great gazongas. Like big, soft, round water balloons, bobbing all over the place when she walks.

Oh, man, now Rex is waking up. I can't think about Sydney in her yellow sweater and type this thing at the same time. I need to take a break.

Okay, I'm back. So the restaurant was really fancy. Dark red tablecloths, hardly any lights, the waiters dressed up in suits. Sydney ordered this chicken with mole sauce, which has chocolate in it. Gross. Chicken and chocolate together. I just wanted a couple of beef tacos, but she said to get something more interesting. So I had to order this fish thing with its eyeball still on, looking all pathetically at us and costing $6.50 more than the tacos.

Sydney was real friendly to the waiter, telling him about our project. The waiter got Eduardo to come out of the kitchen. He let Sydney take his picture. He explained how he used to work at his mom's restaurant in this little Mexican village. It'll look great for our oral report. If Sydney hadn't been so friendly, we'd never have all this help.

Then Eduardo had his brother the chef come out. Both of them were mega-fat. *Muy gordo,* as they say *en espanol.* Dad says it's good for chefs to be fat because it shows they love food. I don't know. I bet they dip their fingers in the food before it leaves the kitchen.

Eduardo took a picture of me and Sydney with the chef. I put my arm around her. Even though her shoulders are sort of like a guy's because she's on the swim team, I felt really warm because of her yellow sweater and maybe the spicy food too.

After Eduardo took our picture, I left my arm there for like 30 seconds more and Sydney didn't pull away. That was the total high point of my night, of my week, probably even my month and year. And even though this wasn't a date, since it was for school and she drove and we split the bill, it felt like a date during those 30 seconds, and it felt excellent.

Oh no, there goes Rex. I guess I typed enough. Bedtime.

Saturday, February 5

Mom's been a total mental the last few weeks. She's either all tense or she's sleeping. And it's not like anything unusual has happened. Me and Amanda are just our normal bratty selves. Mom doesn't even have law school finals until May. The only thing I can think of is she's coming down with menopause. Isn't that supposed to take a couple years though? I can't handle it that long.

What's really weird is that the more neurotic Mom acts, the happier Berm seems to get and the more he hangs out here. If my girlfriend was always yelling at everyone and falling asleep at 8:00, I wouldn't be coming around all the time.

If Mom and Berm broke up, I wonder if I'd ever see Berm again. He asked me to bowl for the spring league, but what if Mom and him get into a fight or whatever. Would he blow me off? I'm starting to think possibly not.

Tonight Berm came over for dinner, and Mom made this raunchy chicken cacciatore. It was all dried out and the sauce had black burn spots in it. Lucky for Amanda, she was on a date.

I went into the kitchen to make myself a bologna sandwich. Then Mom had a fit. She went on and on about working hard in the kitchen and no one ever appreciating her. Berm and I didn't say anything. I just went back to the table and choked down the rest of my dinner. None of us had seconds, which like never happens, so I'm sure Berm hated it too.

Then Berm started clearing the table, and Mom got mad at him for rushing her. Then she got mad at me for not helping him. So we had to clear and wash the dishes while Mom sat on the couch reading about corporate law.

Next thing we knew she fell asleep with the book on her lap and the highlighter in her hand. It was only 8:26. I thought maybe Berm would go home, but instead he sat on the couch with me and watched the Lakers game. They rule.

At halftime, since the game was such a runaway and Mom was sitting in between us snoring and we were hungry after that awful chicken cacciatore, we drove over to Der Weinerschnitzel and ate some dogs in Berm's Jeep.

I'd love a Jeep. The problem is, by the time the average guy can afford a cool car, he's already too old for it. A Jeep isn't so bad, but when you see like an old bald man in a red Porsche or something, that's when you realize life sucks.

33 hours until driver's ed class.

Sunday, February 6

I'm 15 now. It's not that big a deal. Not like when I turned 13 and became a Man and got $1,935 in bar mitzvah money. And it's not like 16, when I can drive, or 18, when I'll get my own apartment. But at 15 I can get my learner's permit and Dad will start giving me driving lessons. In exactly a year I'll drive myself home from the DMV.

Mom offered to have a party. But I wouldn't know who to ask besides Nate. And possibly Sydney. Anyway, at 15 you don't let your mom throw a party for you. I think, anyway. So Mom said she'd cook whatever I wanted for dinner.

The steak was awesome. I got a big T-bone and did a Fred Flintstone number on it. Aunt Marsha came over. She brought her own grainy vegan thing and kept giving dirty looks to the meat. Mom and her mostly talked about Amanda. Even on my birthday, Amanda gets more attention. Mom was pissed because she hadn't come back from Bulimic Michele's house for the big family dinner.

When the Amanda talk died down, Aunt Marsha asked me whether The Pig called to ruin my birthday. Mom gave her a look, like I told you not to call him a pig. I went, "No, he probably forgot. He's probably screwing his latest bimbo delight."

Aunt Marsha started clucking and stuff, and Mom gave me these meaningful glances, like maybe she was thinking, My ex is such a pig, it's all his fault I have such a mopey son. I told everyone to lay off. There's nothing worse than people feeling sorry for you, especially on your birthday.

The night just continued to bomb from there. Aunt Marsha baked one of her barfy nature food cakes, full of wheat germ and shredded vegetables. I had to eat it because it was for my birthday and because Mom kept kicking my foot.

Amanda finally came home with Bulimic Michele, who totally pigged on the roughage-cake. Anyone who could eat that has to have serious eating problems.

While I choked down my piece of cake, Mom did the dumbest thing in the universe. She goes into the kitchen and whispers into the phone. About a second after Mom comes back to the table, the phone rings. She tells me to pick it up. I'm thinking, Why don't we let the machine get it, like we usually do during dinner. Then I pick it up, and it's Dad saying happy birthday. You don't have to be Einstein to figure it out. Couldn't he have waited like maybe 5 seconds after Mom called him?

Monday, February 7

Driver's ed was totally lame. Spent 45 minutes learning about curb colors. I thought I'd learn how to drive.

Got home from school to find Mom laying on the couch crying over this news show about animal shelters. I definitely can't take 2 years of her with menopause.

Tuesday, February 8

Nate came over after school today. We're going to lift weights 3 times a week. This summer we'll be total babe magnets at the beach. Or at least not embarrassed to take off our shirts.

When I dragged the weights out from under my bed, I practically choked on all the dust covering them. Underneath was a dead grasshopper. We worked out for 30 minutes exactly, sweating like pigs. It felt great.

Amanda barged into my room to laugh at our scrawny bodies. Nate's so lucky he doesn't have a sister. In 7 months she'll be out of here, hopefully as far away as possible. Living in some dorm room, dating all the college dudes, hardly ever coming back home. Maybe Mom will let me turn her room into a weight room. If we put a TV in, I could watch while working out.

Soon my shoulders will be bigger than Sydney's.

Wednesday, February 9

I never knew I had so many muscles. Every puny one of them is killing me. I might as well have jumped into an empty cement mixer or thrown myself in front of a tractor, or called the football team a bunch of queers. And for all I'm going through, I don't see one speck of muscle growth yet.

Called Nate tonight at 8:00 to see if he felt thrashed too, but his mom said he was sleeping.

Saturday, February 12

Awesome night, but I'm tired. Spent an hour and 43 minutes cleaning my room before Sydney came over to work on our report. Found $1.42, that math homework I searched all over for last semester, and half a sandwich that might have been turkey.

The dinner pictures turned out good. Sydney scanned them in her computer and blew them up. Everyone has a cool computer except me. We're not using the picture with my arm around her. Our cheeks look really red in it. I wish I wasn't too wimpy to ask her for a copy.

After we finished the report, we just talked. About Spanish class, swimming, cars, books. She's read every novel Edith Wharton ever wrote. I dropped that I'd read *War and Peace* over winter break. She said she liked a man who could read Tolstoy. A *man*. When I showed her my complete collection of S. E. Hinton novels, she said "Wow" like she was looking at football trophies. Of course I didn't mention my other collections—the box of comic books in my closet or the Scrabble stuff hidden under my bed.

She volunteers at the Boys and Girls Club once a week. I asked her what she did there, hoping to hear the word *Scrabble* or at least the words *board games*. But she just helps with their homework.

It seemed so noble, I couldn't mention Golden Village. The whole nursing home volunteer thing sounds good, I guess. But then I'd have to admit I only go whenever I feel like it, and usually talk to only one guy, who mostly just kicks my butt at Scrabble.

I sat on my desk chair, but she lounged on my bed with the pillow propped between her back and the wall. I should get rid of that Batman pillowcase I've had since I was 7. I kept picturing me on top of her in the bed, both of us naked. Luckily I kept Rex under guard. In my vision I was all muscular. Me and Nate better keep lifting weights.

The only bad part was when Mom came into the room Even When My Door Was Closed, with this sudden need to put away laundry. Oh, and also when someone started hurling chow in the bathroom. I explained to Sydney that Bulimic Michele must be over, but I'm sure she got totally grossed out. Listening to those ralphing noises killed any shot of kissing Sydney on my bed. Not that I would have gotten up the guts to kiss her anyway.

Sunday, February 13

Dad's bimbo delight used the word *fabulous* 13 times tonight. Fabulous arugula, fabulous chorizo, fabulous presentation of the sashimi-feta-risotto stack. All in all, a fabulous restaurant, for fans of minuscule portions of weird food. I'd kill for a Whopper right now.

Looked up back journal entries and calculated that just 3 months ago I asked Dad not to bring his girlfriends along on Sundays. Miss Fabulous came the last 3 Sundays. It's just getting worse with him.

Maybe once I'm all muscular and start driving, I'll seem almost like a friend he wants to do stuff with. I could join his gym and lift weights with him and check out the girls in their exercise bras, and maybe hang out afterward at the juice bar. Does Dad's gym have a juice bar? They always do on TV. I'm not going there until I'm in better shape.

Monday, February 14

Nate and I really planned to work out today. But then Nate didn't feel like biking over here. I lifted by myself for 5 minutes, rounded up from 4. I only quit so I wouldn't be sore for the oral report this week.

Amanda got 6 Valentine's Day cards, flowers from 2 different guys, and a box of chocolates from a secret admirer. What do they see in her? I mean besides that she's beautiful and popular and smart. She threw away the candy because she's on a diet, but when I came down to watch TV tonight, I saw her digging it out of the trash.

Berm came over and gave Mom a teddy bear. She cried again. I don't think that's such a great gift. Definitely not worth crying over. Isn't she old for stuffed animals? Maybe she's going through a midlife crisis.

I got absolutely nothing. No candy, no presents, not even a card. The usual. I wonder if Sydney got any valentines. Maybe I should have bought her something. No. Look what happened after I spent all that money on Gina. But Sydney's a lot different than Gina. Thank God.

Wednesday, February 16

Duke really helped me today. As soon as we laid out the Scrabble board, I asked him the question that's been bugging me for 3 days: Do most gyms have juice bars or is that just a TV thing? He said as far as he knew, they didn't. His old gym just had a drinking fountain that was out of order half the time.

Then he said I looked glummer than the lady he ate breakfast with who just had her legs amputated. I told him I'd been hoping I could lift weights with Dad and hang with him at the juice bar afterward. Instead of just going out to eat with him and his bimbo delight every other week.

Then he started acting like a prosecutor, asking me all these questions that I think he knew the answer to all along. I bet he was a great D.A. before he retired.

He says, "Whose idea was it to go bimonthly?" I told him, "My dad's." "And you want more?" he asks. I nodded. He cocked his shaky head and frowned at me.

I said I wanted to lift weights with him, and maybe take up a sport so he could root for me at the games. Then Duke goes, "Like your older sister? Does he root for her?" I said she doesn't talk to him anymore. Then he asks, "But did he used to?"

It hit me. Big time. That Dad never did much for Amanda either. Even when he lived with us, he never hung out with her or anything. What he did for Amanda was bang her assistant gymnastics coach. "Never," I told Duke. "He never even rooted for my sister in gymnastics. Or in anything."

He didn't have any more questions. Just sat in silence while I stared at the Scrabble game for a long time. I was so weirded out, I didn't even notice how much time. I didn't notice much of anything. Just the letters blurring on the board and the sour smell of old people dying as I thought about Duke's questions. As I finally realized Dad never rooted for either of his kids. No matter how athletic or popular or smart or good-looking we are.

After Duke reached out and patted my shoulder, I put down *atlatl*, which he'd used on me back in the fall, and Duke goes, "Good, you're learning."

I guess all this time I've been going about the Dad problem the wrong way. All this time I thought there was a solution.

Friday, February 18

Our report went great. Me and Sydney made a good team. I wore a sombrero, and she wore this little sheer white blouse that I guess was supposed to be like a Mexican peasant outfit. It made her gazongas look huge.

Everyone laughed when we showed the close-up picture of my mouth full of food. I aced the speech I wrote in Spanish. I even threw in the word *arraba* just to show off my perfect *r* roll. Ms. Padilla clapped really hard for us and went, *muy bueno*. We'll definitely get A's.

After class I gave Sydney a high five. Then she gave me a hug. I don't know if it was a just-friendly-teammates hug or something else, but it sure felt good.

Then after that, Robby Poloski tapped me in the hallway and goes, "Nice job, Storky." I gave him my Vin Diesel look, which I've only done before in the privacy of my own bathroom mirror. I said, "The name's Mike. Or Michael to you." As they say *en espanol,* I got *cajones*.

Friday, February 25

Oh, man. Oh, man. Oh, man. I can't even write about this. The whole day all I've been thinking is, Oh, man.

Saturday, February 26

I think I can write about it now. But let me just write Oh, man one more time. Oh, man.

Okay, here's what happened. Yesterday morning we

were all downstairs getting ready for school. I was pouring out my Froot Loops, and Mom and Amanda were packing their lunches. Amanda asks her why she doesn't drink coffee anymore. Mom says she buys it at school now. Then Amanda asks her why she doesn't wear jeans anymore, and Mom says she gained some weight. Then Amanda asks why she gained weight. Mom says she was eating too much. Then Amanda goes, "It seems like all you ever eat these days is licorice and saltines." Mom says, "What are you getting at?" Then Amanda says, "I'm getting at that you got yourself knocked up."

Then I dropped the milk carton. It was nearly full. Almost a half gallon of milk all over the floor. Me and Mom went nuts trying to clean it up, getting out the mop and sponges and paper towels. Meanwhile, Amanda just leaned against the fridge, going, "It's true, isn't it? I can't believe you didn't use birth control."

I felt like I was in a bad dream or a trance. It was too bizzotic to be true. I stared at Mom's stomach, and she didn't look pregnant. I thought, Maybe she's not. Maybe she'll say Amanda's crazy.

But Mom started crying while she mopped. She's like, "Howard and I were going to sit you both down and talk about it," and Amanda goes, "I heard you puking again yesterday. How dumb do you think I am?"

Then I realized I must be dumb, since I figured she had menopause. I didn't ever imagine her getting pregnant. She's 40. 40½, actually. And I don't want to think about how she got knocked up.

Amanda said we had to go so we wouldn't be late for school. I never got to eat breakfast. She didn't even finish packing her lunch. I didn't talk to Mom about it yesterday morning, since Amanda was my ride. I couldn't speak anyway, being like in total shock.

The whole way there Amanda went, "I knew it, I knew it" while I just slumped in my seat, saying, Oh, man to myself about a million times.

BAD THINGS ABOUT MOM BEING PREGNANT
1. Every time I look at Mom, I'll have to picture her having sex.
2. If anyone at school sees her in a few months, they'll know she had sex.
3. Nate will laugh at me.
4. If Mom goes into labor when I'm around, I might have to help her and see her privates.
5. I won't be able to turn Amanda's room into a TV room. It'll be full of cutesy baby stuff and dirty diapers.
6. If Mom has a girl, then I'll really be surrounded by them.
7. Verm will be over all the time.
8. Verm might never come over again.

GOOD THINGS ABOUT MOM BEING PREGNANT
None.

Sunday, February 27

Finally got a reaction from Dad. Not a good one, but something. Progress, I guess.

He was only 22 minutes late tonight. After he picked me up, he got Miss Fabulous at her house. Actually a dinky apartment she shares with this other actress. She brought a little pink suitcase with her. It's bad enough I have to think about Mom having sex. Now I have to think about Dad doing it too. He made me sit in the backseat, even though I'm like 9 inches taller than Miss Fabulous and get squished.

I couldn't wait to tell him about Mom. I don't know why. Maybe so he'd know she's moving on. That she's not the sob queen she was when they divorced. Maybe I wanted to burn him too. Let *him* picture Mom doing it with another guy. Maybe it was just so I could tell someone. I don't know.

I didn't even do a buildup. Just shocked him with it at the Belgian restaurant. "Dad. Mom's pregnant." He was sipping Evian water, and it spilled all over his hand and into his leek soup. I should have waited until he drank his red wine.

He goes, "Are you sure?" I couldn't help smirking. I said, "Do you think she'd have any reason to lie about it?" He didn't answer, so I asked if he was okay. He had to clear his throat before he could say, "Of course I'm okay." The water still dripping from his hand definitely gave him away. Seeing Dad all upset was almost worth Mom getting pregnant.

No, it wasn't.

Monday, February 28

Mom and Dr. Vermin have it all planned out. Everything's settled. Verm came over to discuss it tonight. Except it wasn't a discussion. It was an explanation. It wasn't even that. It was a briefing.

They never once asked me what I thought of all this. I'm getting a stepdad and a half-sister or -brother, and it's all supposed to be this wonderful thing. Mom goes, "I'll take a year off from law school so you'll get to see me more." Like what a wonderful treat. And it's supposed to be so wonderful to go to their wonderful wedding in the wonderful spring.

When people tell you something will be wonderful, when they sound like an infomercial trying to convince you of it, then you know it won't be wonderful. That it'll suck.

Amanda's pissed too. She called Mom and Verm sleazeballs, and ran up to her room. At least Amanda gets to escape to college this fall. Me, I'll be living here another 3 years and 5½ months, in this wonderful house with all these wonderful people I never asked for, ever.

Wednesday, March 2

Duke doesn't think it's wonderful, but he pointed out some positives. He says babies are chick bait. He didn't say it that way. He goes, "Gals flock to young men holding babies like a drunk to Robitussin." Supposedly if I take the baby to school during cheerleading practice, the girls will be flipping and jumping all over me. He also said he hopes the baby turns out just like me. I told him I wouldn't wish my hair on anybody.

Duke said he wished he'd had children, because then he wouldn't be stuck at Golden Village, eating crummy food and playing gin rummy with a bunch of geezers every day. Being so old must totally bite. We're both stuck living with people that bug, but at least I get out of the house most days. I'm taking him to a Padres game when I get my license. Even though he keeps killing me at Scrabble.

Friday, March 4

Aunt Marsha came over tonight with her new girlfriend. Not a total hottie like her old one, but pretty cute. She's got good taste in women.

They were all over Mom, rubbing her stomach, giving her these teas that are supposed to help morning sickness, acting like it's so great to be pregnant when you're 40½ and not even married. That's why I'm in my bedroom typing this lame journal instead of downstairs eating ice cream with everyone else.

I thought if anyone would know how not wonderful it all is, it would be Aunt Marsha. Even Nate says it's not so bad. He thinks it's funny. Yeah, easy for him to laugh.

Maybe he could live here and I could go live with Nate's mom at his house. I know his mom's an alky, but at least she already had menopause so she can't wind up pregnant. But their house is so smoky. Anyway, Mom would never let me.

Sunday, March 6

I guess Grandma's on my team about all this. Not exactly a good thing.

When she came over for dinner tonight, Mom and Vermin told her the wonderful news. Grandma said some mean stuff that I never thought of, like if Mom gets remarried, Dad won't have to pay her alimony anymore. And how Mom will be almost 60 when the baby graduates from high school. And how she wasted 2 years in law school because she'll never work as a lawyer now.

Mom said in this wimpy voice that she hoped to graduate and work part-time, and that Vermin would cut back his dental practice to help out. But Grandma just rolled her eyes and gave a huge sigh. Huge meaning it practically depleted her body of all air. I'm glad she's not my mother.

Mom started crying. It's weird how she acts like a little kid around Grandma. Of course she cries a lot these days anyway. I guess she's got it pretty bad, with Grandma yelling at her, and her kids pissed off, and barfing all the time.

Tuesday, March 8

This is really sick. But I can't help thinking about it. Nate says you can tell when Verm and Mom did the deed by counting back 8½ months from the due date. So being a perv, and good at math, I counted.

They made the baby right on New Year's Eve. The night

I said it was okay for Vermin to sleep over. *I* did it. I mean, not really. They did it, of course, but if I hadn't been Captain Sensitive about Verm sleeping over, they'd never be getting married and having a baby and ruining my life.

I bet they kept all the condoms or whatever at Verm's condo. They probably figured Mom wouldn't get knocked up just from one time at our house without protection. Didn't they ever take sex ed in school? They should give a talk at the middle school about how they messed up their lives by not using a condom.

Wednesday, March 9

The "Spring Flings the Thing" posters are driving me crazy. The student council people plastered them all over school today. I just want to walk around with a marker, putting apostrophes in the word *Flings*. This makes me either very sensitive or a complete nutjob. I bet no one else even noticed the apostrophe problem.

Should I ask Sydney to the Spring Fling? Nate says I should. He thinks she's totally into me. I don't know.

CONS

1. At this point in my pathetic life, the last thing I need is her turning me down.
2. I'm broke.
3. I haven't danced with anyone since December, when I went to Aunt Marsha's.
4. I still have bad memories of the Snowball.

PROS

1. At this point in my pathetic life, what I need is a date with Sydney Holland.
2. I could earn $8 an hour this weekend.
3. I practiced dancing a few weeks ago in front of Amanda's mirror when no one was home. Thought I was pretty good.
4. Maybe I could finally kiss a girl.

Verm wants to hire me and Nate on Saturday to help him clean up his condo. He has to get it ready for the big open house so he can sell it, move in with us, and destroy my life.

Nate really wants the money. I could use the $8 an hour, but I don't want to hang with Verm all day. Plus, by getting his place cleaned up I'd be helping him shack up with Mom. Something really creepy about that.

Thursday, March 10

After being up from 1:46 A.M. to 4:18 A.M., and talking to Nate during lunch, I made 2 decisions. One, I'm asking Sydney to the Spring Fling. I'm tired of being a wuss. Two, I'll help Verm with his stupid condo on Saturday. Just for the money so I can pay for the dance.

Now, how do I ask her? Great. Figuring that out will probably keep me awake again tonight.

Saturday, March 12

Earned $52 today. Me and Nate spent 6½ hours cleaning Verm's condo. We had to straighten out his garage, pack all these boxes for Goodwill, wash the windows, everything. Verm's a real slob. Not like Dad the Neatfreak. At least Verm won't be after me and Amanda all the time to clean up our stuff. I hope not, anyway.

Didn't find much real interesting. No *Playboys* or ladies' clothes or anything. He had a box full of bowling trophies that we tossed. Leafed through his high school yearbook. I was right, he was a real geek back then. He had short hair cut above his ears when everyone else had long hair. Plus he was in the honor society and the science club.

One thing I really wish I hadn't seen is Verm's bed. It's a waterbed. Now I have to think of them sloshing around in it all the time. Gross!

Sunday, March 13

Duke had a stroke.

He looks horrible. Someone from Golden Village called me this morning, and Mom took me to the hospital, and he was just lying there, not moving, hooked up to all these machines like a fly caught in a spiderweb.

He never wanted to be like that. He said to shoot him if that ever happened. I sat next to his bed staring at him, thinking, I don't know how to use a gun and I'm not even sure how to get one. When it comes down to it, I doubt I could kill anyone anyway.

I started crying, and Mom gave me this huge hug. I said, "I don't want to crush the baby," but she said it was okay. I felt like a little boy. For the first time in a long time, I was so glad Mom was around.

I told her Duke didn't want to live like this, lying in a hospital bed all wired up to machines. Then she showed me the Do Not Resuscitate order hanging from his bed. So if his heart stops, they won't shock him with those paddles or anything like on *ER*. They'll just let him die. I guess he got everything set up before he had the stroke. He's so smart. Was so smart?

He never opened his eyes the whole time we were there. I guess that's good, because I could barely look at his face. I felt almost embarrassed for him, lying there being stared at.

Mom kissed him on the cheek, but that was too weird for me. When she went out to find a bathroom, I gave his shoulder a pat and said how much I appreciated his advice on Scrabble and other stuff. Then I started crying again, so I just stood there gripping his shoulder until Mom got back.

Visiting Duke today was probably the worst thing I've ever had to do. I don't want to think of him in that spiderweb bed. I just want to picture him putting a 7-letter word down on the Scrabble board with that big obnoxious smile on his face.

Felt so bad, I canceled on Dad. I had to explain who Duke was. Dad called me Champ when I told him what happened. He said not to worry. Right.

Monday, March 14

Nate's a good friend and all, but he doesn't understand about Duke. He keeps telling me I'd better ask Sydney to the Spring Fling before anyone else does. I guess he doesn't realize how bummed I am, that I can't act all macho and stuff with Sydney and plan out what to say to her when I keep thinking about Duke.

My brain just has no room for the Spring Fling. With Mom being pregnant, Dr. Vermin getting ready to move in, and Duke lying near dead in a hospital bed, everything's spinning in my head like a Hot Wheels car racing around one of those yellow tracks.

I don't care what Nate says. Or who asks Sydney out. Well, I do care about that. But I'm going to wait to talk to Sydney about the dance.

I need at least a week. I'll ask her on Friday, March 25. Unless Duke gets better before that. Who am I kidding? Oh, God.

Tuesday, March 15

Mom offered to drive me to the hospital again tonight. I just couldn't go. I feel like a pig, but I didn't want to see Duke looking like death again.

I hope other people are visiting him. He seems like someone who enjoys having company. Maybe there's even another teenage guy he played Scrabble with. He might even go to my school. We're probably both so embarrassed about visiting an old geezer and playing Scrabble, hardly anyone knows but Duke and me and the other kid.

Mom wanted to buy flowers. I thought it was too girly. So we ended up sending this balloon bouquet that looked kind of cheesy but was better than flowers. Mom tried to hug me, but I moved away. Last Sunday's hugfest was enough for a long time.

There's no other teenage guy who visits him. I'm a jerk.

Wednesday, March 16

Went to see Duke. Guess I grew a backbone last night.

I want to write how he's getting better, how he called out my name or blinked in this big significant way like in a TV movie. But really he just laid there. It's hard to type this. He looks so bad. He needs to die soon.

I guess in a TV movie he'd coach me from the hospital to win the world championship in Scrabble. Actually something cooler, like kickboxing or surfing. And everyone would be so impressed, I'd get totally popular and have a big love scene with Gina at the end.

At least I got a little better at Scrabble though. At least I got to know him. At least I got up the guts tonight to hold his hand in the hospital and squeeze it tight, even though he never squeezed back.

Friday, March 18

Duke died last night. His heart stopped and they followed that Do Not Resuscitate order. The first thing I thought when Mom told me is, Now I don't have to visit him this weekend. I'm a pig. Duke dies and I just think of myself. I guess I'm glad he doesn't have to suffer and all that. But really I'm just a selfish bastard who's happy he's gone so I don't have to look at his half-dead face and his raggedy old body.

Man, I'm crying. I can barely see the monitor. The real truth is I already miss him, even though he was just an old geezer who gave me Scrabble tips. But also he was someone I could always bike over to see. Who gave me advice not just on how long to hold the *s*'s and blanks and where you could put a *j*, but on girls and families and school and stuff. Who said anyone would be proud to have me as a son. Oh, God. I have to stop typing.

Sunday, March 20

I thought this would be a really sad day because of the memorial service, but actually it wasn't. I mean, deep down I feel totally bummed. Glum, as Duke used to say. But for most of the service I smiled or laughed. Maybe it's because old people are so used to everyone dying on them, or maybe because they don't get out much. But Duke's friends mostly joked around, almost like we were sending him off on a cruise instead of to heaven or wherever he is.

Most of the people at the service were real old, all slumped over in their wheelchairs or the cheapo plastic chairs in the Community Room at Golden Village. I kept wondering whether they were imagining their own memorial service. When you get real old, maybe you think about death 97% of the time. Like when you brush your teeth, if you still have any, maybe you say, What's the point, I'll be dead soon anyway. Or maybe you refuse to think about dying, because it's way too depressing. Maybe everyone at Golden Village thinks they're the person who'll live to 120.

Learned a lot about Duke today. I guess he was kind of the life of the party, if you could call living at Golden Village a party. This one little old man said Duke hired a stripper for his 90th birthday. She came into the cafeteria dressed as a nurse, and next thing everyone knew she was sitting on the dude's lap in a G-string.

This lady with no teeth said Duke told her she was the prettiest thing in all of Golden Village, and she believed him until she heard him say the same thing to Fat Frieda, who I guess is dead now too. Then another old lady waved her cane and shouted that Duke told her she was the prettiest thing in Golden Village. We all cracked up so bad, the blue-haired lady fell out of her wheelchair and this old man had to get out his inhaler.

I did more of a serious speech, about how great a Scrabble player he was and how he always listened to me. Then I got carried away by everyone else, and said Duke had great tips for getting the girls.

I know I spent the day with a bunch of old geezers in an institution remembering our friend who died, and maybe it's pitiful, but it was the most fun I've had in a long time.

Tuesday, March 22

That memorial service kind of cleaned out my brain so I'm not constantly thinking about Duke anymore. More like 88% of the time. Now I guess I can decide how to ask Sydney to the Spring Fling.

Still don't have a plan. I should have that cabdriver invite her, the one who asked Gina to the Snowball. Hahaha.

First of all, where do I ask her? Spanish class is too crowded. I don't need 30 other people hearing me get rejected. I could go to school early and hang out by the pool while she's at swim practice. But if she's in her bathing suit, I might not be able to concentrate. Strike that idea. I could wait for her at her locker, but that could be just as crowded as Spanish class. Maybe I could pull her aside at lunch, like Nate did when he asked Heather to the Snowball. Or I could call her. But that seems so wimpy since I see her in school every day, like I'm too much of a wuss to look at her when I ask her.

I think lunch is the best idea. She only eats with one person, Miranda Moran, so it's not like a whole bunch of girls will be laughing at me. Only Miranda and Sydney will.

Okay, lunch. But what should I say? First I have to make small talk. I could complain about the Spanish midterm, and maybe tell her I like whatever she has on. According to Amanda's Cardinal Rules of Dating, you should always give a girl one compliment. More than one is phony and desperate, but girls like to hear one good thing.

But what if Sydney's wearing like a plain sweatshirt and jeans? I can't really compliment her on that. I could say her hair looks good. Except she almost always wears it the same way, back in barrettes, so a hair compliment seems fake.

Maybe I should just get right to the dance question. First I'll ask if she's going. If she is, then I don't have to invite her and get turned down.

If she says she's not going, I'll ask if she wants to go with me. Straight out? Or maybe more subtly, like, If I invited you to the dance, what would you say? Or, Do you enjoy school dances like the Spring Fling? Or, Do you have any other plans on that night?

Okay, so I ask her 1 or 2 of the above questions about the dance. And then if she still acts interested, I hit her with the direct question. Would you like to go with me?

Wednesday, March 23

Got all psyched up to ask Sydney today. Even wore my loose shirt that makes me look like I might have muscles. Walked over to where Sydney usually eats lunch.

She wasn't there. Miranda said she had an optometrist appointment. There's that old Michael A. Pomerantz luck again.

Thursday, March 24

After all that work outlining my 7-step plan to ask Sydney out, I completely blew it. It's Robby Poloski's fault. Sort of.

I got messed up when he and Sydney blocked the doorway into Spanish class. They both acted all dramatic that they were going to bomb the midterm. Like Robby Poloski ever got less than an A on any test, and like Sydney hasn't already spent a million hours studying for it.

Then Robby goes to Sydney, "You have such a great laugh." It's like he was stealing my plan. First small talk about the midterm, then the compliment. And Sydney's laugh isn't so great. It's an ordinary laugh. I just knew he'd start talking about the Spring Fling next.

I stood against the wall listening to them flirt, thinking how Robby isn't good enough for Sydney. Sure he gets great grades, but he has greasy hair and he always raises his hand at the wrong time. Just when the teachers drift away from the subject matter and get interesting, like in history class when Mr. Ellis said how he went to college just to get out of the Vietnam War, or in geometry when Ms. Pinkstaff was complaining about calculators ruining American education. As soon as I start getting into their stories, Robby Poloski's hand shoots up and he asks if it'll be on the final.

Plus I get great grades too. I'm the *man* who read *War and Peace.* I wrote that big speech in Spanish about the restaurant, and I had Sydney over to my house, and I tried to talk to her at lunch yesterday. Just thinking about all that and watching Robby laugh at everything Sydney said, fake as a laugh track, got me so pissed.

Luckily, we all had to take our seats before Robby could mention the dance. The whole class period I kept my eye on him, making sure he wasn't passing any notes to Sydney. I also worried that since he sat closer to her than I did, he'd get to her first after the bell rang. He could easily walk her to her next class and ask her to the Spring Fling on the way, leaving me out in the cold. I could just picture Nate going, I told you you should have asked Sydney last week, acting like he knows so much about girls.

So I decided I had to pass her a note. It's a wuss way to ask a girl to a big dance, but it was quick. I thought of writing a note with my 7 steps on it. Like, I hope the midterm's not too hard. I like your belt. Are you going to the Spring Fling? Do you want to? How about with me?

But I didn't want to make a huge deal out of it. So in the end I just wrote, "Sydney, would you go to the Spring Fling with me, and dinner before? Sincerely, Mike." Then I folded it 4 times, put her name on it, and passed it off.

She read it with a total straight face. She didn't nod or smile or roll her eyes or anything. So I had to sit through the whole next 26 minutes of Spanish class totally stressed.

When class finally ended, Robby Poloski started talking to this glitterbag girl in front of him. He probably wasn't even going to ask Sydney to the dance. I could have stuck to my original plan.

Sydney walked up to me at my desk and said, "I'd love to go with you." Those were her exact words. She said *love*. I think I turned red again. But by the time I started blushing, she'd already headed out the door.

So even though I screwed up my 7-step plan, I was still gutsy enough to ask her and she said yes. And love. If Duke was here, he'd probably be doing wheelchair wheelies, bragging that he knew there was a suave guy inside me just waiting to come out.

Sunday, March 27

Big day. Dr. Berm moved in. First he dropped me and Nate off at the Convention Center for the car show. He bought our tickets too. It was obviously to get rid of me while he took over my house, but we had a great time. They had this babe from some soap opera there. I never heard of her before, but she looked totally hot. We got her autograph. She just signed her name inside a heart on my Jaguar brochure, but Nate got her to write, "Nate, you're my man" on his arm.

They had awesome cars. Nate's into the little hot dog ones, so we looked at the new Porsches for like 15 minutes. I prefer something beefier. I think Jeeps are really cool, even though Berm has one. His is green though. I'd definitely get mine in black.

After Mom drove me home, I had to see Berm all sweaty, unloading boxes. Even though I hate him being here, we have a lot more cool stuff now. Another TV, for one thing. A 25-incher. Not a big screen like I really want, but much better than our 13-incher. They're putting his TV in the living room and the little one in Mom's room. I mean *their* room.

He let me have his chair. A Chargers director chair— blue and yellow, of course, with the official logo on it. It's excellent. I don't know why Mom didn't want it in our den.

I wonder if he misses his condo. But he seemed pretty happy today. Yeah, moving into Mom's bedroom, having sex with her whenever he wants. Though maybe you're not supposed to do it with someone who's pregnant. Like it would be really gross if your johnson touched your baby.

The best thing is his new computer. He's hooking us up to the Internet first thing tomorrow. Awesome! We're keeping the old computer in my room, so I can still type this journal in private.

The other thing that happened is Dad took me out to dinner. He wanted to go to this French restaurant in Del Mar, but I said I should have some choice in the matter. And he actually said okay. So we went out for pizza instead. Miss Fabulous wasn't there, but that's not because Dad wanted to see me by myself or anything. She was acting in a play.

Dad asked me about Duke, but he called him King. He said, "How's King doing?" I don't know why, but I laughed so hard, and I kept laughing when I said, "He's dead, Dad." Dad looked at me like I was nuts, and I went, "Duke, Dad, Duke. Not King." He didn't think it was funny. I guess it's not.

Oh, I didn't even write the major thing that happened with Dad. When he came to pick me up, Berm was still moving all his stuff in. Dad always parks at the curb and honks so he and Mom don't have to talk to each other. Which is much better than the old way, when he came to the door and did all that awkward small talk with Mom, and they tried to sound like they barely knew each other. Half the time it turned into a fight. Mom would say, "You're late again," or Dad would tell Mom how messy the house looked, or Mom would tell Dad he was 2 months behind on child support. Sometimes they'd stand there yelling so long I'd just go up to my room and close the door. I guess it helped me see maybe the Divorce wasn't such a bad idea.

When Dad pulled up, Berm and Lester from the bowling league were standing in the driveway, about to get this big box out of Lester's truck. Berm walked over to the Lexus and shook Dad's hand. He was only over there like a minute. I watched it from my bedroom window. I wonder what they said to each other. So you're the one who knocked up my ex-wife? So you're the one who made her cry all the time? Weird.

When I came out, Berm gave me this big wave and goes, "See you later," like trying to show Dad how tight we are. I didn't even wave back. I just went, "Bye" real quietly.

As we drove to the restaurant, Dad gave me the FBI treatment. Did he sell his place? Do you get along? Does Amanda like him? Is he divorced too? Does he work full-time? A lot of talking for Dad.

I couldn't tell if he was pissed off or sad or just curious. Or maybe he was deciding whether he could cut back on the child support and get Berm to take over. I bet Dad's really jealous, thinking what a mondo mistake he made moving out, and how it's too late now to do anything about it. Or I might just hope that.

Would I even want Dad back? Maybe it's better to have the imaginary Dad in my head who shows me how to drive and buys me a Jeep, than the real Dad in my house who complained about our noise and our school papers lying around and never seemed happy unless he was on his way out the door.

Monday, March 28

The Internet is awesome! Been on it 14 hours today except for short food and bathroom breaks.

Thursday, March 31

Here I am in the Chargers chair typing in my bedroom. I can't believe spring break is almost over. I spent it in front of the new computer. I even found a site where you can play computer Scrabble against other people.

Mom's freaking out. I told her she should be happy because I'm not watching so much TV anymore. She's not happy. Tomorrow the new computer's going in her room, and I'm only allowed an hour a day on it.

That sucks, but in a pathetic way I needed someone to get me away from the computer. Nate's pissed because I didn't want to hang with him much this week. Plus I was supposed to read *Moby-Dick* for Honors English and I didn't even pick it up. And I should have been planning what to do for the Spring Fling with Sydney.

Oh yeah, Amanda decided where she's going to school. University of Arizona. 6 hours away. I bet she only comes home like twice a year. I might even miss her on rare occasions. Probably not though. Maybe I can visit her and get tickets to Wildcats games and sleep in a coed dorm and go to frat parties and meet drunk sorority girls.

Friday, April 1

Berm has lived here exactly 5 days.

GOOD THINGS ABOUT DR. BERM MOVING IN
1. He cooks dinner and the food's a lot better now.
2. Mom stopped wearing her stained bathrobe with the rip under the sleeve.
3. Amanda's home now even less than she used to be.
4. He brought all this cool stuff with him.

BAD THINGS ABOUT DR. BERM MOVING IN
1. It's creepy to watch them go into Mom's bedroom at night.
2. I had to see Berm in his bathrobe this morning. He's so hairy.
3. He does this morning cough/spitting thing that's totally disgusting.
4. He finished off the last apple cinnamon Pop-Tart, the Doritos, and all the leftover Chinese.

Saturday, April 2

I feel really weird about what happened tonight. Can't decide if I'm an idiot, a jerk, or someone who finally got smart. I'm leaning toward the last one.

It started out like it did 4 months ago, but ended a lot different. I was watching the new 25-inch TV. E! did a show about some modeling contest. I got this great idea to mute it while I listened to *Sports Talk* on the radio.

Everyone else was gone. Amanda's sleeping over at Bulimic Michele's house. Make that Formerly Bulimic Michele. Her big spring break trip was to some eating disorders clinic in L.A. Mom and Berm went to the symphony. One good thing about Berm being here, he can get dragged to that stuff. When Mom took me last year, I spent most of the night wondering if someone could actually die of boredom.

So the phone rings and I go, "Hello," and there's this silence. I go, "Nate," thinking he's playing a belated April Fools' joke on me. Then a tiny voice goes, "It's Gina." She has this little high voice anyway, but it was even softer than usual. I got all psyched up. I couldn't help it. Then she said, "Mi-i-i-ike." Just like that other night she called, and I pictured her holding the phone with one hand, wiping her eyes with the other, her mascara all runny just like last time when I picked her up from Denny's.

I felt sorry for her and kind of happy to hear her little voice, until she said that I was the third person she called, that everyone else was out, that she and Hunk had this big fight at Pizza Palace and she told him to leave and he did, and that she was stranded again. I guess I was supposed to rescue her.

I half listened. Not only did I think about how she'd blown me off, but I also wondered who the other 2 people she called before me were, and why Hunk and Gina would go to Pizza Palace, which is all grungy-looking and has that crust that tastes like cardboard. I didn't ignore her on purpose. It's just that there was so much about Gina I hadn't thought about in so long. And because I had other stuff going on too. The other stuff namely being Sydney Holland.

When Gina stopped crying about Hunk, we were silent. I knew she wanted me to come get her again. But this time I didn't feel like it. No one was home to drive me, and I wasn't going to blow the money I made at Berman's condo for cab fare.

So I didn't say anything. Gina was all quiet and I started to feel guilty. I thought, Maybe she's too choked up to talk. Maybe she's about to start sobbing. I said, "What are you going to do?"

Then Gina goes, "Can you come get me?" She said it in a bitchy way, like I was too stupid to see the solution, like she couldn't believe she had to point it out.

I told her Mom and Amanda weren't home. I didn't feel like going into how Berm was living in the house now too, so I just said Mom and Amanda. I said I could wait until they got back, that maybe one of them could drive me over.

Then Gina goes, "Never mind." Her voice had lost all traces of sweetness. It sounded like any ordinary person's. Or actually, like a spoiled, nasty person's. I said, "Why don't you call your folks or a cab?" And Gina goes, "Yeah, okay, good-bye." Then she hung up.

So that's what happened. I don't know if Gina will get back with Hunk or how she got home from Pizza Palace. I hope she's all right. I doubt we'll be friends anymore like we were. But we hadn't really been friends for a long time, and that wasn't a good type of friendship anyway—me moping after her, her always asking for favors, telling me about the Incredible Hunk, and probably psyched up to be the object of a crush.

I just feel so weird about it all tonight. Like I wrote before, I don't know how I *should* feel. But what I *do* feel mainly is proud of myself for sticking up for something for a change. And really wanting to go to the Spring Fling with Sydney, who I think likes me as much as I like her.

Sunday, April 3

Spent all day cramming for the driver's permit test. My brain's filled with numbers—maximum speeds, alcohol limits, traffic fines. 35 more hours and it'll all be over. I better pass.

Monday, April 4

Studied so hard for tomorrow's DMV test I didn't even watch TV. Last night I dreamt I failed, and Nate and Amanda and Gina all pointed to this big red F on my test and laughed like crazy, and Dad kept shaking his head and said, You'll never get behind the wheel of my car, in fact you'll never even sit in the front seat.

Tuesday, April 5

Got my permit! Scored 100% on the test. Of course I studied hard enough for it. Drove Mom to the dry cleaner's, the bank, and the watch-repair place. It was awesome.

Mom's too paranoid to let me go on the freeway. I don't know if it's because she's pregnant or what, but she sure is a stress case. She kept going, "Slow down, slow down," and doing these loud gasps and slamming her foot on the floor like there's a brake on the passenger side.

When I see Dad on Sunday, I'll arrange some driving practices. He's a much better driver than Mom. She's always doing the exact speed limit and looking in her rearview mirror. Dad's really good at changing lanes on the freeway all the time and honking so he doesn't have to be behind slow-pokes.

Wednesday, April 6

Sydney and I were the first people in Spanish class today. It was kind of weird. Like we were both very shy. Couldn't think of anything to say, so I asked her if it was supposed to rain. What a dork. But then she went on and on about the weatherman on Channel 8, and her yellow umbrella, and how the clouds looked. I guess we both get geeky when we're nervous.

Nate came over after school. We opened a can of Pringles and pigged. Instead of Mom bawling us out for eating junk food before dinner, she had some chips too. In fact, Mom ate more than we did. We finished 2 cans. She's getting fat. Nate says it's like her boobs are pregnant. I told him to shut up.

Sunday, April 10

I had it all pictured in my head: practicing parking and U-turns at the Best Buy lot that's usually half empty, driving on the freeway on weekend mornings, learning how to change lanes without slowing down too much.

All night at the stupid French-Vietnamese restaurant, I hinted about driving lessons. Saying, I got 100% on my permit test, and Mom's all paranoid in the car, and You drive so smoothly, Dad. He either didn't get what I was leading up to or pretended he didn't. So finally when we shared that gross green squishy thing for dessert, I had to ask him straight out in front of Miss Fabulous. I went, "Dad, remember you said you'd teach me to drive? What days are good for you?"

Dad didn't even pause before saying, "No days." He just brushed me off like I was a time-share salesman calling at dinnertime. I never thought he'd turn me down. I thought maybe he'd say he could do it only once a week or something, but not that he would never do it, not at all. I didn't think he'd say he couldn't spare the time.

He offered to pay for driving lessons, which I guess in his mind solved everything, but to me wasn't the point. The point is he only wants to see me twice a month, and only if his girlfriend tags along. The point is I should have known he'd say no, I should have known better. I should know how he is. I hate how he is. I hate Dad.

Tuesday, April 12

Oh, man! I didn't know any of this was going to happen today. Today or any day. Duke never even hinted about it.

We went to see Duke's lawyer today. I didn't even know he had a lawyer. Mom picked me up after school and we went downtown to a big law office on the 14th floor of this ritzy glass building. The lawyer treated me like an adult—shaking my hand, calling me Mr. Pomerantz, talking to me instead of Mom.

She said, "Do you know what Mr. Jacoban left you?" I went, "You mean Duke, he left me something?" She handed me this copy of his will with the part about me highlighted. It said Michael Allen Pomerantz and it had all these legal-type words, real official looking. And it said he was giving me $30,000 that I had to use for a car and insurance. *Had to.*

I let out a loud, "Oh, man" in the lawyer's office, and started smiling and couldn't stop. I'm smiling now as I type. $30,000! For a car! This is so excellent!

Duke never told me he was going to do this. I didn't even know he had that much money. Enough for $2,000 to each worker at Golden Village, except the nurse he called Miss Misery. Mom and some of the other volunteers got $2,000 too. Plus he gave $200,000 to San Diego State.

Maybe he did it so the thought of dying wouldn't be totally heinous. He was so smart. It's just one more thing that makes me miss him even more. I miss him a lot, but oh, man, I'm still grinning just thinking about the awesome car I'm going to buy.

Wednesday, April 13

WHAT I'LL NEVER DO AGAIN AFTER I GET MY CAR

1. Beg Mom and Amanda for a ride.
2. Listen to Mom's Soft and Easy Hits on the radio.
3. Breathe in Nate's mom's cigarette smoke.
4. Take a bus.
5. Pay for a cab.

WHAT I CAN'T WAIT TO DO ONCE I GET MY CAR

1. Make Amanda beg me for a ride.
2. Turn the radio on to my station as loud as I want.
3. Cruise around with Nate looking for cute girls.
4. Just drive without going anywhere.
5. Take Sydney on a date.

Thursday, April 14

Bought *Car and Driver* and a cool Lakers key chain. Found some good car sites on the Net. Asked Mom to get me a price quote from her insurance agent. Only 298 more days until I get my license.

Saturday, April 16

Maybe with Dad how he is and Duke gone, there's some weird karmic reason for Berm in our house.

Though if someone was put on Earth to guide me, it wouldn't be a fat dentist. When I came downstairs this morning, he was watching a sports bloopers show on the flowery couch in his old plaid bathrobe, a bag of pretzels on his lap. I guess I'd have been grossed out a month ago, but now I'm getting used to him. In a way it's good to see another slob like me.

Mom had already gone to the law library, and Amanda was out somewhere being popular. So that left just me and him. Berm's like, "So what are you up to today?" And I thought, Great, now I have 2 people on my case about lying around the house. I shrugged. I didn't have any plans, and if I did, it was none of his business. Berm goes, "We could drive out to this great steak place in Ramona." *We* meaning him and me.

It sounded like a decent idea. I hadn't had steak in a long time. Not with Dad, that's for sure. He's too busy eating yuppy chow. And Mom's always cooking girly food like baked chicken and broiled halibut.

Then Berm asked if I wanted to drive. For some reason, I never thought of driving with him. But since Dad said no, and Mom's all nervous, Berm seemed like a pretty good option. Actually about the only option. So I said I'd go.

He was an okay driving instructor. Not paranoid at all,

even when I cut off this old man getting on the freeway. Plus Berm's Jeep is totally cool. You can feel like every bump on the road. Berm said I could get one for under $30,000. He looked all proud when I asked him. I didn't have the heart to tell him I wasn't buying a Jeep because of him. It's just that I like Jeeps. I'd get a black one anyway, not green like his.

The restaurant was awesome. The steak was so huge I almost didn't finish it all. They served great onion rings too, a greasy mound of them stacked about half a foot high.

On the way home Berm got mushy on me. It's like he planned it. Like he had all this stuff to say and he set up the road trip so he could get it out. He said how happy he is to be living with us. "All 3 of you," he said. And how the wedding will be the best day of his life because Mom's the best thing that ever happened to him. When he said that, he got all choked up. I didn't look at him because I had to concentrate on the road. Besides, I didn't want to.

I didn't say anything, but he kept talking and talking. He said Mom did a good job raising me and Amanda. Then he goes, "And your dad, of course, too." Which we both know is a lie, since Mom did like 97% of the raising while Dad was off working and screwing around on her.

He said that he likes me and Amanda, and that he doesn't want to put me out. That he hadn't meant for things to happen so fast, but they did. Then he stopped talking.

He probably hoped I'd say I wasn't put out, that I'm really into the wedding and the baby too. But that isn't true. Berm's okay and all. In a way it's good to have another guy around. But in another way it's not. I didn't want to lie and say how wonderful it all is for me. So I just gave him this lame thanks. Then I asked him how fast you should go in the fast lane and how often you should look in the rearview mirror, just to break up the weirdness of the drive.

After he answered my driving questions, he goes, "Mike, there's something important I want to ask you." I told him to go ahead. So he cleared his throat and threw me a glance and said, "Will you be my best man at the wedding?"

My first thought was he was just trying to get me on his side about marrying Mom, so we'd be this big happy step-family. But then he said, "It would mean a lot to me," and his voice cracked like it really *would* mean a lot. I said, "Sure" in a casual way, because I'm not one of those people who like big mushy scenes.

Except I was feeling mushy. As we got off the freeway, we passed the bowling alley, which seemed like some more weird Berm karma. I asked him, "Whatever happened to that bowling league you wanted me to join?" He goes, "They moved it to Sundays, it's starting next month, but I know Sunday's your night with your dad, so I didn't mention it." I couldn't help sighing.

I pulled up to the house and we sat in the driveway awhile, even after I put the car in park and took the key out of the ignition. Neither of us made a move to get out. For one thing, I was so full from all that steak and onion rings, but for another I guess we were just enjoying the car and the man stuff.

Finally I looked out my window at nothing and said,

"Can you take me out driving again, like once or twice a week? Maybe around the Best Buy parking lot or on the freeway early in the morning?"

I could feel his hand reaching out and then roughing up my hair, which was okay just this one time. I turned my head toward him. He had a goofy grin on his face, as if he couldn't wait to teach me to drive. As if he didn't mind that I'm nerdy and don't do much besides watch TV and type this journal and read my Scrabble dictionary. As if he likes that. As if he just likes me. He said, "Great idea. What days are good for you? Wednesdays and Saturday mornings okay?"

I nodded, because I didn't think I could talk.

Sunday, April 24

Dad flaked again. Says he has some important meeting at Qualcomm. What's the point of missing out on the bowling league if I don't see Dad most Sundays anyway?

I called Sydney to ask what color her dress is so I can match a corsage to it for the Spring Fling. Very sensitive of me. Also I wanted to hear her voice. She has a great telephone voice. Peppy and sexy at the same time.

She goes, "It's a light lavender dress with thin spaghetti straps, so a wrist corsage would probably be best." Rex liked hearing about Sydney's thin straps. I had to distract him by listing the planets of the solar system.

I still managed to say, all suave, "I'm really looking forward to the Spring Fling." She said, "Me too," and then there was this awkward silence. Finally, Sydney goes, "It'll also be a relief when they take down those annoying posters."

I almost dropped the phone. Okay, I did drop the phone. But I picked it up again real fast. "Because of the apostrophe problem?" I asked her. "Yeah," she said, "I knew you'd notice too."

I think I've found my soul mate.

Friday, April 29

The Spring Fling's 23 hours away. Only 21½ hours if you count dinner beforehand. Only 21 hours if you count what time Sydney's picking me up.

I'm ready. I ordered the corsage, tried on my suit, and made reservations at Hawthorne's. Sydney's driving, but that's okay. I'm paying for everything. Just the white orchid corsage alone set me back $26.87.

I'm not that nervous. Not like before the Snowball. Maybe it's because I've already been to a major dance and I know the Spring Fling can't be anywhere near as heinous as the Snowball. Maybe you need one really bad dance to get out of your system, so other dances won't freak you out.

WHAT I LEARNED FROM THE SNOWBALL

1. Don't go out with anyone on the rebound.
2. Make reservations for dinner.
3. Don't think you can use coupons on the sly.
4. If a pretty girl keeps pulling up her strapless dress, don't take your eyes off her.

Sunday, May 1

I did it. I did it. I did it. I kissed a girl. I kissed Sydney Holland. With tongue involvement. More than once. It was excellent.

The first time I kissed her, we were slow dancing to some cheesy Mariah Carey song. Or maybe it was Vanessa Williams. Or Whitney Houston. Whatever. While we danced, we stared into each other's eyes just like in the movies. Sydney looked so beautiful in her sparkly dress and with her cheeks all red. I told myself, It's now or never. I bet I said it 18 times.

But I did it. I put my hands in her hair and I kissed her. And she kissed me right back. It was just before the song ended, but we spent the whole next song like that, swaying around and kissing to some hard-rock thing. We stood in the middle of the dance floor with all these other kids around us, but I didn't care who saw.

In fact, I hope people saw. I hope they said to themselves, Old Storky isn't such a geek after all. Maybe they thought, We shouldn't call him Storky anymore. Let's change his nickname to Romeo, or Smooth, or just stick to Mike.

Anyway, I'm never answering to Storky again. I'll tell anyone who calls me that to lay off. Unless it's like a really huge guy.

But back to the important stuff: my kissing Sydney. At first, when I put my tongue in her mouth it felt pretty gross. But then I got used to it. Her braces didn't even hurt my tongue. More like tickled. And besides my hands getting all sticky from the hairspray or whatever in her hair, it felt awesome.

We danced so close I could even feel her nipples against my chest. I don't think she wore a bra. I tried to remember every winner and runner-up of *Survivor* just to keep Rex in line.

Then we got some cookies. I wiped my face with a napkin, because it was all slobbery. Then we sat on the white folding chairs and started kissing again.

Actually, after a while it got kind of tedious, but I didn't want to break it off and be rude. Amanda should add that to her Cardinal Rules of Dating: Don't kiss someone for more than 10 minutes. Sydney turned her head away first because she had to sneeze. I wonder if it was a fake sneeze. Maybe she was bored too.

Nate didn't go to the Spring Fling. Neither did Gina. Not that I looked for her. Well, maybe a little. Hunk went. With Heather Kvaas. They danced to the slow dances and everything. I wondered whether Gina knew, whether she was home crying or maybe even trying to call me. But it was just like a 2-minute thought. In this horrible way I thought Gina deserved it, and Heather and Hunk deserved each other. But that was only like a 90-second thought. Mostly I was thinking how great Sydney was, and how the Spring Fling ranked right up there with my bar mitzvah as one of the best times of my life.

We kissed again in the car when Sydney dropped me off. She rubbed my back under my suit jacket, and her fingernails felt all sexy, and Rex snapped to attention. It was dark, so I don't think she noticed. Anyway, she's already seen Rex like that once before.

When I got in the house, I took off my jacket, held it in front of my suit pants, and started listing countries in Africa. But everyone was asleep by then anyway. Guess I'm the party guy of the family now.

Well, not totally. On the way home from the dance I promised to volunteer with Sydney next week at the Boys and Girls Club. Won't that be a wild date.

Thursday, May 5

I'm getting a brother! After school Mom dragged me to her doctor. I didn't want to go, but she said that it would be good for me, and that I had to if I wanted a ride to Sydney's swim meet on Saturday. Amanda said she'd come out of curiosity, but she was bringing a book.

So me, Mom, Amanda, and Berm crowded into this little room. We watched the nurse check Mom's blood pressure. Amanda read *Ravish Her Gently* the whole time. Berm asked the nurse all these paranoid questions, like whether Mom's blood pressure was too low and if she'd gained enough weight. Earth to Berm: Mom's turned into a blimp. She's gained enough weight.

I didn't have much to do except stare at the walls. Actually, I couldn't stop staring at the chart showing how big a lady's privates had to stretch to get the baby out. The circle that was supposed to be the actual size of the stretched privates was like the size of a Frisbee. Ow. I'm glad I'm a guy. They should just bring that circle to sex ed classes and no girl would ever get pregnant.

When the doctor finally came in, he had Mom pull her pants down a little. I looked away, but Mom goes, "Relax, you can only see my belly." Not only is Mom's stomach humongous, it has blue veins bulging all over it.

The doctor did a sonogram of Mom's stomach, like a cross between a video and an X-ray. He moved the camera around Mom's belly and we all stared at this monitor. We could see the baby.

It was the most awesome thing. He held his little johnson like he was playing with himself, and everyone in the room laughed. The doctor goes, "It's definitely a boy," and Berm got all mushy. I did too, but kept it to myself. Berm actually cried and shouted, "It's a boy!" like 8 times. We got to see his tiny heart beating and count his fingers and toes. At the end it looked like he waved good-bye to us. I said, "See you in a few months," and everyone laughed, even Amanda.

I wonder whether he'll look like Mom or Berm. I hope Mom, for his sake. And whether he'll get all excited when I come home from school. Maybe he'll clap his hands or drool or something when he sees me. Maybe his first word will be Mike. That would be so cool. I should secretly teach him my name every day until he can say it.

Maybe he'll be as smart as me, and I'll lend him my favorite books when he gets older, and we can have big intellectual discussions about them while Sydney admires the bond between Captain Sensitive and his brother Lieutenant Compassion.

His nickname will be Lieutenant, but his real name will be Mason. Mason Pomerantz Berman sounds excellent. I'll try to get Mom and Berm to name him Mason.

I know he'll be a pain in the ass, waking me up all the time and stinking up the house with his dirty diapers. But seeing him today, live, made me think about the good parts of having a little brother. I won't be the youngest anymore, not by a long shot. And I can play with him. Like give him shoulder rides. When he gets older, I'll explain girls to him. As best I can anyway. I could even teach him about kissing now, and how to drive. Just like Amanda taught me her Cardinal Rules of Dating, I'll think up my own Cardinal Rules of Life.

Sunday, May 8

When I asked Dad to change the time he sees me so I could bowl in the league, I didn't expect him to say no. Just like the driving lessons. I always thought that because he's my dad he should be a certain way. That he should *want* to take me driving and stuff.

Maybe I've been watching too many *Brady Bunch* reruns. Maybe that's the real problem with TV. It's not the sex and violence. It's that there aren't any crappy parents on the air. So anyone with crappy parents in real life thinks they must be doing something wrong.

But they're not. It's not their fault. Look at Nate. He's not a bad guy, but his dad practically disappeared on him. And even Mom. She gets all stressed cleaning and cooking every time Grandma comes over, but Grandma disses her no matter what.

So I realized something tonight. Not just tonight. It was dawning on me for a long time. Duke helped me figure it out. This is what I know now: It's not about me. About how I am. It's just how he is. It's that Dad is selfish, not that I'm unlikeable. I bet even if I was star pitcher of the varsity team, he'd still say he couldn't switch times to see me, that Sunday at 6:30 was the only time he could do it.

So I'm joining Berm's Sunday night bowling league. If Dad can't find another time for our visits, then he'll have to wait until the league is over. I told him that too. When he said, "I don't know if I can arrange that, Champ," I just answered, "Then it's your loss." Which I know now is true.

I also know that even if he moves the visit times for me and leaves his bimbo delights at home, things won't change that much. He'll still show up late and take me to trendy restaurants and not bother to learn the names of my friends. I know that's just how he is.

Strange, but as I'm typing this, I'm feeling better. Like I was in the smoggiest part of L.A. and now I'm breathing ocean air in San Diego. Or like I felt last week after I got up the nerve to kiss Sydney and she kissed me back. Like I really am the star pitcher of the varsity team and Dad's some assistant coach who didn't want to let me play.

Saturday, May 14

Mom's getting married tomorrow. I guess you're supposed to feel pissed off when your mom gets married to someone who's not your dad. But I'm not mad. I kept trying to feel pissed off today, but I couldn't. I guess Berm's grown on me.

POSSIBLE REASONS WHY BERM'S GROWN ON ME

1. He brought over the 25-inch TV, the Internet hookup, and the Chargers chair.
2. He makes sure there's beef jerky in the cupboard and Cheez Whiz in the fridge.
3. He put up with Mom turning psycho when she got pregnant.
4. He's teaching me to drive.
5. He didn't act too mad yesterday when I dented his bumper parallel parking.
6. He got all excited when I said I'd be on his bowling team.

I don't know what it is. Probably a combination of things. Old Berm just got to me during the last 9 months. Like *Invasion of the Body Snatchers*, but in a good way.

Sunday, May 15

Mom and Berm tied the knot today. It wasn't a big fancy wedding. They had the ceremony in the backyard and lunch afterward in the house. The only people there were the rabbi, our family, Nate, Formerly Bulimic Michele, Aunt Marsha and her girlfriend, Grandma, Lester from the bowling league and his wife, and Berman's older sister, who flew in from New York.

Berm's sister is kind of chunky like him. I wonder whether Mason will get Berm's fat genes or the Pomerantz skinny genes. Hopefully he'll get a mixture and be just right.

Last night I had this deranged dream that when Rabbi Markowitz did the Speak Now or Forever Hold Your Peace speech, Dad jumped over the backyard fence and said he wanted Mom back, that he wanted all of us back, that he missed living with Mom and me and Amanda. Then Berm took out a giant dental drill and nailed him right in the forehead, making Dad fall backward into the wedding cake.

I woke up all sweaty. I guess you never totally get over wanting your parents back together, even if you just have bizarro dreams about it. The rabbi didn't even do that speech. Maybe he was worried Grandma would scream out a ton of objections.

I don't think Grandma smiled once. Amanda said it was hard to tell what freaked Grandma out more—Mom waddling down the aisle in her maternity dress, or Aunt Marsha dancing with her girlfriend after the ceremony.

Amanda stayed in her room with Formerly Bulimic Michele until right before the ceremony started. But once she came down, she acted pretty decent. She didn't even bring a paperback with her. Me and her were Beast Man and Maid of Horror, as Amanda calls it.

After lunch, she made a toast. She said how Berman was good to Mom, and even though they were both old, they seemed like teenagers in love.

I wonder if it was just bull. Maybe Amanda decided that since she's leaving for college in a few months anyway, she might as well act nice.

After Amanda's toast, everyone stared at me. So I stood up and wished Mom and Berm luck. Then I joked that they wanted to make sure of their fertility before they tied the knot. That didn't go over too well. Grandma even closed her eyes and put her hand on her forehead like she had a migraine. Then I said how Mom seemed real happy now, and I gave her a hug.

I was about to sit down, but something came over me. I went over to Berm and hugged him too. He hugged me back like I was his long-lost son just returned from the war.

Then something else made me do more of the toast. Maybe it was just a way to get out of that long hug. Not really though. I faced everyone and said, "And as for Dr. Berman, if I had to have a stepdad, I couldn't do much better than Berm." It wasn't supposed to be funny, but people did that isn't-he-a-cute-kid laugh. Totally annoying. It's true though. I really doubt I could do better than Berm. If I had to have a stepdad.

After all that, it was a relief to go to my room with Nate and drink the leftover champagne he'd swiped from the kitchen. Nate wants me and Sydney to fix him up with someone on the swim team. Not a diver. According to Nate,

87% of all divers are lezbos. But swimmers are supposed to be easy.

I doubt Sydney is easy though. I think she's a virgin. I hope she is. What if she isn't, and she's sick of just making out with me? Probably once you do the deed, you can never go back to just kissing. She seems to really like just kissing. I bet she's a virgin.

I'm going to call Sydney right now and tell her about the wedding and stuff. We've talked to each other 7 out of the last 9 nights. Tomorrow we're going back to the Boys and Girls Club. I'm teaching this 7th grader Scrabble fundamentals. I wonder if Sydney could be considered my girlfriend. That would be cool.

Monday, May 16

CARDINAL RULES OF LIFE (FOR MY BROTHER MASON WHEN HE GETS OLDER)

1. Just when you're sure your life perpetually sucks, your life will turn totally awesome. But it'll probably suck again soon.
2. People who say high school is the best time of your life are wrong. I hope so, anyway.
3. Behind every night spent drinking with your friends is a hangover waiting to happen. Usually it's worth it.
4. Watch your aim. You won't go blind, but you could mess up Grandma's hand-knit afghan.
5. One sign a girl doesn't like you is if she only calls

when she needs a favor. Another sign is her making out with another guy in front of you.

6. Someone who doesn't seem cool at first can be cool. Even a poetry-loving old geezer or a lesbian dancing queen.

7. Mom and Berm will warn you to wear a condom. Listen to them. They know what they're talking about for once.

8. Next time you think how great it would be to have a dad like Mike Brady or the *Home Improvement* dude, remember, Mike Brady never had kids in real life and the *Home Improvement* guy did time for dealing drugs.

9. Life is like Scrabble: It's not how many *s*'s and blanks you pick, but what you do with them.

10. If people call you a stupid nickname or treat you bad, know that you deserve better. If they keep doing it, send in your big brother.